The Gold Standard

VIBE *a Steamy Romance*

Series #8

The Gold Standard

Lynn Chantale

4 Horsemen
Publications, Inc.

The Gold Standard
VIBE a Steamy Romance Series #8
Copyright © 2023 Lynn Chantale. All rights reserved.

4 Horsemen
Publications, Inc.

4 Horsemen Publications, Inc.
1497 Main St. Suite 169
Dunedin, FL 34698
4horsemenpublications.com
info@4horsemenpublications.com

Cover & Typeset by Autumn Skye
Edited by Blair Parke

Library of Congress Control Number: 2022951979

Print ISBN: 978-1-64450-787-2
Audio ISBN: 978-1-64450-789-6
Ebook ISBN: 978-1-64450-788-9

Dedication

When I started this series, it was to show that blind/ visually impaired people could do anything most sighted people can do. There are even things in the books I tried to poke humor at because these are comments or situations we face on a daily basis. You would be surprised at how often someone will say, "Oh, you don't look blind." Or when asked where the bathroom is someone will point and say, "Over there." There are even times when a sighted person will try to help us sit in a chair or put our seatbelt on for us. I've even had someone offer to help me wipe in the bathroom. And most recently, someone asked if I needed help putting on my belt in my pants.

Yes, these are all things that have happened and will happen again. Sitting is easy; finding the chair in an unfamiliar location is a challenge. Putting on a seatbelt is easy. And most of us have been wiping our own butts since we were three. We bake, cook, clean, dress ourselves, put on makeup, raise children, hold public office, have fulfilling careers, own businesses, and guard our independence with fierceness. If you're not sure what type of help a VIP may need, ask them. If you want to know how we do what we do, ask. Oh, and if you see one of us out and about with a guide dog, remember don't talk or touch the guide. Doing so is a distraction, and you could potentially harm both handler and dog.

First, thank you to everyone who helped in the making of this book, my publisher, editors, and those whose brains I picked for research. Also, I'd like to take a moment to say a special thank you to Southwest Florida Council of the Blind. They are a fantastic bunch, and I'm so glad to be able to call them friends.

Finally, for the readers. Thank you for joining me on this journey. You have truly made it memorable.

Table of Contents

Prologue

Troy Curtis smiled as he wheeled up next to the trim man dressed in a dark wool coat and fedora. The hat was pulled low, keeping the man's feature shadowed. Both trailed behind a plump, older woman in a sleek navy blue pantsuit. She proffered a key to a barred door.

On the other side of the bars were rows and rows of floor-to-ceiling safety deposit boxes of all shapes and sizes. She held the door open, allowing Troy to propel forward; his companion stepped in behind.

Knowing the procedures from past visits, Troy wheeled toward the waist-high wood drawer, parked the handbrake on his wheelchair, and stood. Using the cabinet for additional balance, he scrawled his name on the line, then turned to the woman, key in hand.

She took his key and hers before inserting both into a 10x12 box on his left and just shoulder height of the bank employee. She removed her key.

"Would you like me to remove the box or bring it into one of the privacy rooms?" she queried.

Troy shook his head, as he carefully made his way the scant three feet to his box. He carefully removed the container, leaving his key. With barely a sigh, he sat back down, preparing his body as pain ricocheted up and down every nerve ending in his body. He only breathed as he released the handbrake and turned his chair. They made their way to a privacy room, and Troy placed the container on the counter. He waited until the door closed before he addressed his friend.

"Are you sure about this, Danta?"

His companion, Danta, loosened his scarf as he nodded, revealing full lips with a hint of a smile. "This is the only way." He pushed his hat back.

Now Troy read a mixture of concern and sadness in the hangdog eyes. "You told me to keep this for an emergency." He placed his hand on the closed gray-green box. "Are you sure you want to play this? There's no going back."

"Everyone who knows about this is either dead or incarcerated."

"Like you," Troy quipped.

Danta nodded. "I'm doing this to protect the ones I love."

Troy opened the long metal flap. He sifted through his will, the deeds to his home, birth certificate, death certificates for his parents, a few mint condition baseball cards, old stamps, coins, a gold brick, several silver and platinum bars no bigger than a bar of complimentary hotel soap, and, finally, to the small, padded envelope. He hesitated for just a moment before removing two of the small bars.

"If you're really in trouble, you'll need this." He pressed the metals into Danta's palm.

He smiled. "You're good family, Troy, but I have enough." Carefully, Danta returned the metal to the box, but pocketed the envelope.

"I thought the guy you were dating was some sort of cop."

"Private investigator," Danta clarified.

"And he can't help you?"

"He is, has and does." Danta readied the scarf around his face, then tilted the hat to cover the rest of his face. "He's got babies due any day, and I don't want to be responsible for bringing any more heat to his family."

Troy closed the lid, before placing the box on his lap once more. "If the heat dies down, will you be back?"

"Missing me already?"

Troy chuckled. "You're all the family I have left. I wouldn't even be in this chair if not for you," referring to the car accident that left Troy in constant pain.

Danta shook his head. "You'd have made it where you are without me." Danta opened the door, which Troy rolled through first. Upon seeing them exit, the bank employee rose from her seat behind a long curved counter, walked through a chest-height locked door, and met them at the entrance to the safety deposit box vault.

This time, Troy handed the woman his box. She returned it to its spot, closed the door, and then returned to him his key.

"Thank you, Virginia," Troy called as he rolled from the vault.

"My pleasure."

Together, he and Danta moved from the bank into the blustery cold of winter in Ann Arbor. They paused on the sidewalk adjacent to the parking lot.

"If there's anything I can do, you let me know," Troy said, his warm breath misted in the cold air.

Danta nodded. "I will, cousin. Stay safe and thanks."

As Troy rolled to his vehicle, a full-sized SUV modified with hand controls, he observed his cousin walking to the opposite end of the parking lot. He watched as Danta pulled the envelope from his pocket, opened it, and slid out something wrapped in silver foil. Troy squinted. *Is that a stick of chewing gum?*

Standing, Troy folded his wheelchair and stowed it in the back. Slowly, he walked to the driver's side door and slid gratefully into the still warm leather seats.

Why would his cousin have him store a piece of chewing gum in his deposit box?

Chapter One

The sweet aroma of chocolate, cinnamon, and warm yeast greeted Troy as he rolled into PB & J Bakery. A bald black man, in a pale blue apron emblazoned with a peanut butter and jelly sandwich on the bib, offered a quick nod of acknowledgment as he slid several cherry- and chocolate-topped cupcakes into a waiting box. Troy returned the greeting as he waited his turn.

He perused the glass cases full of cookies, cupcakes, individual pies, cakes, and other pastries as he waited. By the time it was his turn, Troy had his choices narrowed down to a crème brûlée and a couple of the chocolate croissants.

"Hey Troy."

"Avery!" he greeted. "How's it going?"

Avery Cheathams grinned. "Great if I could keep my wife out the kitchen," he said loud enough for a red-haired and very pregnant woman to hear.

"Penelope, it's Troy."

Penelope placed a tray of chocolate and fruit tarts on the top of the case.

"Hi Troy." She blew a wisp of hair from her face. "I miss coming to class."

"Miss having you there."

"You were only supposed to work on Geneva's cake, not plate the desserts," Avery admonished.

"Sweetheart, you're shorthanded in the kitchen." Opening the display case door, she hesitated and then traded an empty tray for the full one. "See. Easy-peasy." Clutching the empty tray to her bulging middle, Penelope waddled back through the swinging double doors.

Avery shook his head. "The woman will be the death of me."

"She looks great."

"The important thing is she's happy," Avery told him.

A pang of longing filled Troy. He wished he had a woman he could love as much as Avery obviously did Penelope. For a moment he thought about another woman, her curvy, lithe frame now firmer after the last few months of exercise. He could imagine her hot and sweaty beneath him or, better yet, hot and sweaty over his knee. How he would love to bring his calloused palm down on her supple ass.

"So what can I get ya?"

Troy blinked, realizing he was still in the bakery, and even more grateful his stiffy couldn't be seen from his seated position. To hell with it. "I'll take one of the crème brûlée and two of the chocolate croissants."

⌒

Gold Falls leaned so close to the mirror, her forehead kissed the glass. Carefully, she applied a thin line of kohl to her lower and upper lids. She set the eyeliner aside before she picked up a black eyeshadow with tiny glittering crystals. She brushed a liberal amount to each lid before blending it with a silver shadow. Now she pushed her glasses on her nose, inspecting her handiwork. Satisfied, she turned away and spritzed on one of her fave body sprays. The faint floral scent reminded her of tropical flowers and hot, lazy days, a perfect scent for this blustery winter day.

As she walked from the bathroom, she pressed the side button on her watch. Time was 7:03 a.m. Nodding, she sat on the tiny bench in the even tinier foyer to pull on a pair of warm boots. She still had about ninety minutes before she had to be at work.

Shrugging into her heavy wool coat, she strode into the cold January morning.

Immediately her glasses fogged over. She removed them and wiped the moisture away. Now that she could see again, she stared longingly at an older Jeep Cherokee with about four inches of packed snow on its hood and roof. The 4x4 looked forlorn, abandoned there in its parking space. If she could drive just one more time.

"Good morning," a cheery male voice greeted her.

"Hi Dad." Gold fixed a light smile on her lips. For as long as she could remember, her father, Theodore Falls, was her biggest cheerleader and her greatest protector. She knew his shift started soon, but here he was offering her a ride to work. She wondered if he had an ulterior motive.

Deftly, the older man offered her an elbow, as he led her to the passenger side of a running sedan.

She loved her father, more so now that her mom was gone and he was her only living parent. But she was still curious as to why he picked this morning to play chauffeur.

"No lunch with you today?" he said, opening the door.

"We have a working lunch, so it's being catered." Gratefully, she slid into the welcoming heat of the car. Theodore closed her door as she pulled on her seatbelt.

"You know I could've called a car service to pick me up. You didn't have to drive me into work," she told him.

He strapped on his seatbelt before shifting into drive. "I know, but this gives me a chance to spend a little time with you."

"Really, Dad? Like dinner on the weekends isn't spending time with me? Or teaching me to shoot? Or self-defense?"

He chuckled. "We've had to postpone our usual dinners."

"We've made up for them in lunches or other ways." She shifted in her seat until she could see all of her father's face. The man hadn't quite reached fifty yet, and he was still handsome. Tiny strands of gray swirled here and there in his close-cropped black hair. He'd recently let his beard grow in, and she had to admit it gave him a more distinguished appearance.

"Is it about the shooting?" she asked quietly. A few months before, he'd been called to a scene where he'd been forced to take the life of a suspect. If he hadn't, the four people inside a burning house would not have survived. And two of the four survivors were her patients, but all were friends.

He reached over and squeezed her hand. "Now, Gold, don't start analyzing me. The department shrink has done enough of that."

She winged a brow. "So the great Sgt. Falls actually went to therapy this time?" she quipped.

Theodore chuckled. "Shows what you know; I go to therapy every few weeks. It clears out the cobwebs and makes me a better cop."

"Really?" She couldn't keep the amazement from her voice. She'd known her dad was a bit more progressive than some of his counterparts, but knowing he willingly spoke with a therapist eased her mind, especially since her mom was no longer with them.

He squeezed her hand again. "I see a lot of tragic stuff. The worst things human beings can do to one another. At the end of the day, I don't want to fill the holes in my soul with alcohol, pills, or even a bullet. My Bessie might not be waiting for me at home at nights anymore, but I do have a daughter I love dearly. If anything, I can make the world a safer place for her."

Tears burned her eyes at his heartfelt admission. "Thanks, Dad."

"I've been meaning to tell you; you've lost weight, and you're glowing." He braked at a red light. "I'm glad you got interested in the class your clients mentioned."

Now she squirmed in her seat. How could she tell her father she had a crush on one of the trainers and that was the main reason she kept going to the gym? "I find it helps clear my mind on the days I go."

He nodded. "Of course."

"And I actually sleep better at night," she admitted quickly. "And it's a thrill to finally get in the dress I've had in the back of my closet the past three years."

"The uh," Falls drummed his fingers on the wheel as he thought, "little red mini dress with beads."

"Uh yeah." She swiveled to look at her father. "How did you know?"

"You don't forget the perfect dress when your daughter drags you to every store and boutique within a fifty-mile radius," he teased.

She chuckled. "You loved every minute of it." She smiled fondly at the memory. A little bittersweet. She'd bought the dress for a Valentine's dinner, one she thought would've been a very special night. But the man she'd hoped would've proposed to her, well, he hadn't and the dress stayed in the closet waiting for another special event.

"If there's any consolation, the jerk bag is living way beyond his means out in Chelsea. And if the grapevine is to be believed, his wife is a real ballbreaker."

She turned her head so her father wouldn't see the faint smile curving her lips. The news did send a spark of satisfaction through her. In her therapist mind, she understood this was a perfectly reasonable reaction, but the woman side of her grieved that Evan wasn't even happy with the choice he'd made, and she, well, was happy but lonely. She wanted, no yearned, for companionship, for someone she could come home to at the end of the night and just curl up or snuggle with and relax. If she were really honest with herself, she wanted to experience something only her clients spoke about, things she'd only read and researched but never had the opportunity to try. Staring out the window, she blew on the glass until it fogged and drew a heart in the mist. Then she drew a jagged line down the middle. The drawing was a fair indication of her life now.

"Did I lose you over there?" A note of humor clung to his voice.

"No," she began slowly. "I was thinking not being with him turned out to be a blessing in disguise."

"How so?"

She glanced at her father. That's right, she hadn't told him about the misgivings she'd had about Evan. How it was a bunch of little things, like him not being in the places he said he would be or lying about where he'd been when she had receipts to prove he was elsewhere. She never had proof he cheated on her. She didn't get the vibe there was another woman or man in his life like that, but she had gotten the sense he was hiding something from her.

"We weren't on the same wavelength anymore," she finally said. "Even though the breakup hurt, it wasn't as bad as I thought it would be. I mean I was sad we lost our connection, but not the grieving sadness of losing my best friend and lover."

Falls patted her hand. "Then he wasn't the right person for you," he stated. "When I lost your mom, I forgot how I liked my eggs, couldn't remember how to dress myself, and forget about tying my shoes."

Gold snorted a quick laugh.

"But eventually, I pulled it together enough because I had you to think of. I couldn't let my grief overtake being a parent. Bessie wouldn't have wanted that."

"No, she wouldn't," Gold whispered past the lump in her throat. "I miss her too."

"And that's why I keep my appointments with a therapist. As to say when it's the right one, your heart will let you know."

They lapsed into silence, a shared melancholy settling in the vehicle like a third passenger. Gold reached out and flicked on the radio. Bright laughter floated through the sound system, dispelling some of the gloom.

"Do you have time to stop for breakfast?"

"Stop by PB & J Bakery," Gold said. "They're on the way, and they have great pastries."

Once Falls pulled to the curb outside the bakery, Gold pushed out of the car into the frigid air. She shivered, wrapping her scarf higher on her face, and hurried across the salted walk to pull open the heavy metal and glass door. Chimes rang above her head. Immediately, she was enveloped in warmth, cinnamon, and yeast. Inhaling gratefully, she wiped her feet before traversing the tiled floor. A yellow triangular placard warned of a wet floor. She skirted this and stopped short. Large tires filled her vision.

"...and a crème brûlée," the gruff voice was saying.

Gold gnawed her lower lip. Of all the bakeries he had to wheel into, he wheeled into her favorite one. She sidled a little closer and caught a whiff of man and sweat, along with a hint of something woodsy. His scent always made her a little giddy. The last person she expected to see this bright and early was Troy.

"Hey, Gold," Avery greeted. "I'll be with you in a minute." As he spoke, Avery placed croissants and another pastry in a small box. "You want your usual?"

"Yes, please."

Troy swiveled in his chair, pinning her with liquid brown eyes filled with amusement. "Your usual?" he queried, with one eyebrow raised.

"They have these fantastic breakfast sandwiches," she explained. Realizing what she was doing, she paused. "Not that you really want to know."

He rolled closer before touching her hand, as he gazed into her face. "You look very pretty today."

Gold gasped. Of all the things she thought he would say, telling her she was pretty was not one of them. "Um, thanks." She stared at his hand on hers. Lean, strong fingers gave way to calloused palms. At least they would be calloused if they weren't encased in fingerless gloves.

Avery stepped around the display case. "Here ya go, Troy." He extended the bakery box.

"Thanks." He reached for the box Avery held out. "You coming to class tomorrow?"

"Of course," she answered quickly. "It's why I can eat PB & J's amazing breakfast sandwiches." Face. Palm. How could she say something so lame? Here was a golden opportunity to flirt with the man she'd been crushin' on for weeks, and all she could talk about was food.

Smiling, Troy set the box in his lap, waving away the change Avery offered. "Tip jar."

Nodding, Avery returned to behind the counter and dumped the bills and coins into a gallon-size glass jar already half full of money.

"You've been working hard," Troy said. "There's nothing wrong with a little reward."

He tapped the box in his lap. "See ya' later."

He wheeled out the door, another patron holding the glass as he left. Gold only stared, wondering again why she hadn't said more.

"You want a hot chocolate to go with your sandwich?" Avery cut through her thoughts.

"Yeah. I think I will." She glanced at the case. "Could you box up a couple dozen cookies too? I want to surprise my dad."

Chapter Two

Gold studied the five women sitting in a semi-circle in front of her. They all shared two unique traits: all were blind, and all were self-employed. The women varied in ages from mid-twenties to early sixties. What brought them all together was the same person or sequence of events⊠ someone had tried to kill them and, in some instances, more than once. Gold didn't counsel them so much as facilitated their support group.

Abigail, owner of a downtown bar and eatery, clutched her hands in her lap. The two rings on her left hand winked in the overhead fluorescent lights. At her feet was an aging English Lab. The dog lifted one brow, as if to ask, "Is it time to play?" before dozing off again.

Geneva, heavily pregnant and the youngest of the group, was a social media influencer who had a run-in with a stalker who'd broken into her home. On Geneva's right was Amelia Bedford-Hastings. At her feet laid her guide Kiska, a beautiful black Lab. Amelia operated a law firm. Next to her sat Penelope Bishop, owner of PB & J Bakery. She also was pregnant and looked ready to pop any day, but her due date was still a couple months away.

To Gold's left was August, a relative newcomer to the group. Her guide Riley sat between her feet, nearly nose to nose with Percy. While August was the only one who hadn't been targeted by Mr. VIP or Rodney, a mutual friend to all of them, her attacker was just as close and personal. The final woman in the group, and the only one without a visual impairment, was Greta Gaines or GG, as she preferred to be called. Absentmindedly, she rubbed her right shoulder, almost as if massaging a tight muscle. It seemed all the women, with the exception of Geneva and GG, had been targeted more than once.

"Well, ladies," Gold began. "You all look beautiful and rested. Life is treating you well?"

No one spoke.

"Abigail? Is there something you'd like to talk about?" Gold prompted. "You seem a little tense."

"Just nightmares. They're worse when Swift is out of town, like he is now, but everything else is good," she answered.

"Could you describe your dream?"

Abigail pursed her lips before pushing her hair behind her ears. The last year or so had been filled with so much turmoil and joy. "The bar is doing better, but I'm ready to move on. Do something new. Enjoy the rest of my life with Swift."

"Do you believe wanting to do something new is the cause of your nightmares?"

"I keep dreaming about loss. Of losing Swift, and I can't do that again." Abigail released her hands and flexed her fingers. "More or less, I keep thinking Rodney will come back and finish what he started."

"Me too," Penelope spoke up.

"Especially after he abducted Joshua and Avery," Amelia put in.

Just a few months before, Amelia and Penelope had been targeted by Rodney Kimball. This time, the man orchestrated a prison breakout with two other inmates who had it in for the group of women seated in the circle. Rodney hoped by taking out Avery and Joshua, it would clear a path for Rodney to then murder Amelia and Penelope. Their crime? Being successful business owners as well as loving men who were sighted.

"I still have a hard time believing Rodney was behind so much devastation," Geneva said with a slight lisp. "He was always so kind to me and for him to turn on us."

"It's a sense of betrayal," August stated. "He was a trusted friend. Someone you cared about, visited with, exchanged pleasantries..." She cleared her throat. "I considered David a friend and, at one point, thought I owed him my life for saving me."

She too had been targeted, but by David Foster Marsh. He'd brought his dog Misty to her obedience school for training. In the ensuing months, he'd sent her a bomb in hopes of earning her gratitude and when that didn't work, he tried to kill her. Not once, but twice. Even going so far as trying to murder both her partners and her meta. The sad part was David almost succeeded in taking them out. Not only had he sent a bomb, but also set the house they were in on fire, then stood outside with a gun, waiting to shoot anyone who exited.

"I can't believe the man tried to kill Jason," GG said.

"I still feel guilty about that," August spoke up. "If I hadn't been involved with Jason...."

"The fault is not yours to shoulder," Gold admonished gently. "Your attacker, all of your attackers, chose to vent their frustrations in the most heinous ways possible." Gold looked at each woman in turn. "What I see before me are six amazing women who persevered and not only that but are thriving. You haven't let the chaos of the last few months stop you from living. You've chosen to confront your fears, anxieties, and whatever else ails you and rebuild your lives. The men who love you are willing to do anything to make sure you're happy." How she wished she had a man who would love her the way these women were loved.

She allowed the voices to flow around her, each woman offering encouraging words or a bit of advice. Gold listened with half an ear. She hadn't had any real trauma in her life, not like these women, her friends. The worst she'd experienced was a broken heart, but her training as a therapist and her natural empathy and compassion allowed her to guide these women to a sense of what was normal for them.

Amelia, who had buried one husband, thought she'd buried her current husband, only to learn her family wanted to steal her inheritance. She was thriving and happy. The interlocking hearts at the hollow of her throat winked in the light. One of these days, she'd have to ask Amelia about the necklace. She tuned in again when a burst of laughter filled the air. Gold looked over to find GG with a gooey smile on her face, as she held a hand to Penelope's swollen belly. Even from this distance, Gold could see the movement beneath Penelope's top.

"That is so cool!" GG cooed. "And so amazing."

"What's amazing is there are two of them in there," Penelope said dryly.

"I never get tired of the movement," Geneva chimed in. "Jethro takes every opportunity he can to touch the baby. He's so excited to meet our son or daughter."

"You didn't find out the sex?" Abigail ventured.

"We wanted to be surprised, but I swear I'm having a boy."

"We're having one of each," Penelope announced. "Once we learned I was having twins, I didn't want any more surprises."

A ripple of laughter went round the room. Now the talk turned to babies, breastfeeding, and diapers. Gold allowed her thoughts to wander. What would it be like to have a baby with Troy? A little boy with his dark liquid brown eyes or his caramel complexion. Heat skipped across her cheeks. Where in the world had that thought come from? With effort, she forced her attention back to the women in the room.

"You guys are so tough and strong. There's no way in the world I could do what you're doing," GG was saying. "When I watch Jason, I see how he struggles with some things, but he doesn't let it stop him. Even after his accident, he was eager to return to the kitchen. There are days I'm afraid to leave the house, and our attacker is dead and the other in jail."

"I have days like that too," Amelia readily agreed. "But I don't let the fear rule me."

"You can't," August stated.

"Exactly," Geneva piped up. "We live with blindness everyday of our lives and if we allow someone else to dictate the rest of how we live..."

"We won't live," Abigail finished. "I know there are those who choose to give into their fears, but you're looking at a roomful of women who refuse to give in or give up."

Never give up or never give in. Gold pondered those words as she walked the three blocks to the bus stop. Calling for a car or even her dad would've been easier, but she wouldn't have the time to think. Cold nipped at her nose and cheeks. She re-adjusted her scarf to ward off the worse of the cold. Still, the air permeated through her layers and sapped the heat from her toes and fingers. With a sigh, she jammed her gloved hands into her pockets. At least she had that, and the brisk walk to the bus stop would keep the blood circulating. Hopefully the bus wouldn't be late. Traffic sped back and forth, the slick brick street rimmed in salt was little deterrent for motorists venturing home or more fun places, like dinner or movies. It wasn't late, just a smidge past five-thirty p.m., but Michigan winters were already dark. Streetlights, headlights, and building lights were enough illumination to ward off the nightly gloom.

Gold stepped out of the flow of pedestrians and admired the city. Her city. Ann Arbor was the quintessential melting pot. People from all over the world migrated to the city for school, work, or fun. For a moment, she absorbed the energy.

Her offices were located in an office building across the street in Kerrytown. There was a co-op on the corner; across from that, the building that housed the farmer's market on the weekends and several niche shops the rest of the week. A paid parking lot on the corner diagonal and some sort of bistro was there, as she squinted in the glare. Shoot. She wasn't sure what the place was. Most of the time she had her lunch delivered or brought it with her. She didn't venture out much, at least not since she stopped driving.

If she'd been driving, she would be halfway home by now, not marveling at the night or the pedestrians, some with dogs on leashes. The more woke pet owners had their animals outfitted in sweaters and little boots.

Gold held back a snicker. She could understand the sweater, but the boots. As if to agree with the sentiment, a chihuahua pranced on the sidewalk, looking like it was trying to kick off the little boots affixed to its paws.

"Now, Belle," its owner crooned. "It's to keep the yucky salt off your feet."

The tiny dog wiped at the leash and continued to dance until the owner picked it up. A tiny dog biscuit appeared from somewhere, which the dog eagerly took. Only then did Gold become aware of a vehicle pulling alongside her.

The passenger window buzzed down, and she stared into a pair of liquid brown eyes.

"Need a ride?"

Troy couldn't believe his good fortune. Twice in one day he was seeing Gold. Now all he had to do was convince her to get in the car with him. "C'mon. It's nice and warm in here, and you won't have to wait for your ride." He reached across the seat and pushed open the door. "I promise to keep my hands to myself."

A ghost of a smile flirted at her lush lips. "Like you do in the gym?" she demanded, sliding into the truck.

He waited until she closed the door, then clicked her seatbelt before maneuvering back into traffic. "Are you saying I've touched you in an inappropriate manner?" he challenged.

She spared him a sidelong glance. "If you had, you'd have a weight permanently imbedded somewhere."

He grinned. There was the feistiness he'd come to like and look for. "So, you know my mama raised a gentleman?"

"With the way you torture us in class?" she demanded. "I know your mama didn't raise you to beat up on women."

"No, but she did raise me to please them and give them what they need."

She surprised him by laughing. "You are such a charmer."

He glanced at her at the next red light. She'd removed her hat and loosened her scarf. The long, pretty box braids were wound into a loose knot. He realized he wanted to spend a little more time with her than the drive would allow. "Wanna grab something to eat?"

She stared at him. "What?"

"You know food, prepared in a restaurant and brought to us at a table?"

She rolled her eyes. "I know what food is," she remarked dryly.

"Is it the company you're objecting to?"

She gnawed her lower lip. He'd seen her do this at the gym as well. She was thinking. About him? What having a meal with him would mean? Maybe he could sweeten the deal.

"Would it make you feel better if I said it's my treat?"

"Like a date?"

They were passing two shopping plazas, one on either side of the road. A defunct K-Mart, along with Plum Market, a 24-hour fitness center, and a thrift store, was on the right side of the road, while a branch of the public library, a cupcake place, a restaurant, and Kroger, a local grocery store, were on her left. If they continued this way, they would pass a few more hotels, Weber's restaurant, and a few other eateries.

"My place is closer to the mall."

"That's cool. The restaurant I have in mind is across Zeeb before you get to Scio Farms."

Gold racked her brain for where he could be taking her. "Restaurant on the River?" she queried.

He flashed a quick grin. "You've been there?"

"They make a fantastic French onion soup if you're into that type of thing."

Twelve minutes later, they were seated at a table, perusing the menu, while they sipped on glasses of water. Gold pulled a magnifying glass from her bag to bring the words into better focus. She couldn't believe she was actually here with Troy, like they were on a date. Was this a spur of the moment thing or had he planned on scooping her up?

She shook her head. No, it had to be in the moment. He couldn't have known she would take the bus. Or that she would stop on the sidewalk to admire the night. And he couldn't have known what time she left the office. And if he was driving up and down Jackson Road, watching for her, well, that was just creepy.

"You're thinking awfully hard over there." Troy set his menu aside.

"Was wondering if you were stalking me."

He flashed a grin. "And if I was?"

"You know my dad is a cop," she reminded him.

He nodded.

"And he taught me how to deter unwanted advances."

"Are you always this skeptical?" He wanted to know. "Why couldn't I have been on my way home?"

Gold paused. He very well could've been on his way home, but she had no way of knowing. She didn't even know where he lived. If anything, she knew he was a gym rat, spending most of his days working out. He volunteered with a bunch of other trainers, but what else did she know about this man?

"So, you were on your way home and saw me woolgathering on the sidewalk?" She stared at him across the table. "How did you know it was me?"

Smiling, he waved a hand toward her coat. "You wear the same coat when you come to the gym."

The server chose that moment to return with their drinks, an iced tea for Gold and a lemonade for Troy. A moment later, the server left with their menus and orders.

"I also noticed you weren't driving anymore," Troy began quietly. "Did your Jeep break down?"

Gold flinched; he really had been watching her. "The Jeep is fine. My eyes have gotten bad enough it isn't safe for me to drive anymore," she admitted past the forming lump in her throat.

He placed his hand over hers on the table. "That has to be tough."

She nodded. "It's been an adjustment. In the meantime, my vehicle sits in the lot, mocking me."

"Do you think about selling it?"

Sipping her tea gave her a moment to think. If she sold the Jeep, she could save on insurance. After all, she wouldn't have the payments, but it would signal the end of her independence. The next thing to go would be her license, and she couldn't give that up. At least not yet.

"I'm not ready," she answered truthfully.

He nodded in understanding. She scrutinized him and realized he did understand.

"What's the story of the chair? Did you walk over a land mine?"

"My story would be so much cooler if I had. Nope. A car accident many years ago messed up my spine. Throw in flare-ups from SLE (Systemic Lupus Erythematosus), and I have a seat wherever I go." He patted the arm of his chair with affection.

Gold smiled at the quip, actually pleased he had a sense of humor about his condition. One day, she would be like that with her failing eyesight. She hoped.

He sipped his lemonade. "I thank God everyday I'm alive to do what I do."

A soft smile curved her lips. "Does anything get you down?"

He shook his head, dislodging one of the locs. He pushed the braid from his face. "There's so much negative out there, I truly try to stay positive and help where I can. Which is one of the reasons for the adaptive classes. Too many people with physical challenges think they can't exercise, so we show them they can."

"You do more than just exercise. I've seen you advocate for others."

He ducked his head, an embarrassed smile. "You saw that?"

"It was brilliant. The fact that you were so willing to speak candidly about your personal struggles really helped and shed a lot of light on how society approaches accommodations. Even I learned something, that even though entryways are wider than before, a lot of them still fall short in accommodating wheelchairs with wider tires."

Nodding, he studied her a moment. "What's your fantasy, Gold?"

Her gaze snapped to his at the sudden change in topic. "Um..." Had she somehow projected her fantasy? Did he somehow know she had visions of being bound and spanked? Of being dominated by him?

"Think on your answer very carefully, because I know you're involved in all my fantasies."

Mouth dry at his admission, Gold shifted on her chair, heat tickling all her erogenous zones. Staring in his liquid brown eyes only made the crotch of her panties damper. She crossed her legs in an effort to alleviate the sudden ache. "And if I said I fantasize about you too?" she ventured.

Lust, desire, and something else she couldn't quite identify flared in his irises. "I can work with that."

After the meal was eaten and the check paid, Gold followed Troy from the restaurant. She tried not to shiver when Troy's fingers stroked the back of her hand. He cast a sidelong glance at her, as if gauging her receptiveness. If he told her to drop to her knees and suck him off, she'd gladly comply. The icy night barely registered as they emerged into a cold embrace of the night. "I love the winter," she grinned.

He gazed at her dubiously. "And you like the cold too?"

She laughed. "I love all weather, cold or hot, but the winter is the best." They paused on the corner, waiting for the walk sign to flash. "Sitting in front of a warm fire, snuggling under a fuzzy blanket, and drinking hot chocolate with marshmallows."

"Marshmallows?" he quipped.

"Absolutely."

"Why not a glass of wine or brandy?" They crossed the street.

"Because it's my fantasy."

"What else do you fantasize about, Gold?"

She turned to face him with wide eyes.

In one deliberate movement, Troy braked his chair and stood. With infinite gentleness, he drew her close for a kiss. The cold melted away as he touched his lips to hers. She tasted of salt and sweet from the caramel apple tart she'd had for dessert and a unique flavor all her own. He'd waited for this moment all night. It wasn't enough to touch her hand or sit across from her at the table. He needed to feel his lips on her, his hands in the coils of her thick hair. He grasped a handful, eliciting a moan. Her lips parted, and he deepened the kiss.

He was a little rougher than he intended, ravishing her mouth as she opened for him, yanking her to him as he held her in place.

Gold pushed her hands inside Troy's coat and clutched handfuls of his shirt as his fingers tightened in her hair. Her scalp tingled at the small bite of pain, zipping down her nerve endings to pull between her legs. The man could kiss. He shifted, bringing her closer to his erection. A hand skimmed her back to press her even closer. She felt the outline of him through their layers of clothing, and it excited her more.

He snaked a hand beneath her shirt, pinched the tight bud of her nipple through the lace of her bra. Liquid desire surged to dampen her panties, and she nipped his lip in return.

"You like it rough?" he whispered against her lips.

Her eyes fluttered opened to find him watching her. Lust glazed his eyes, and she knew she had to look the same. A chill swept across them, and she shivered.

What were they doing? Making out in the parking lot of a restaurant like they were a couple of randy teenagers?

Hastily, she dropped her hands and tried to back away, but his hand in her hair and on her breast prevented this.

"You didn't answer my question," he said in the same husky voice.

"I..." She licked suddenly dry lips. The fingers, which had been gripping her hair a moment ago, massaged her scalp.

A grimace rippled over his face. He stumbled backward. Gold clutched at his jacket in an effort to prevent his fall. He fell heavily into his chair, bringing her with him.

"Ow. Oh. Sorry," she muttered, struggling to find her balance.

Troy held her a moment. "Are you hurt?"

She shook her head as she gained her feet. "I should be asking you that question." She smoothed a hand down her clothes, then studied him.

Despite the cold sweat dotted his forehead, she asked, "What happened?"

"Spasms," he admitted through gritted teeth. "Nothing big."

For a long moment, they stared at one another. She waited for him to elaborate, but after a few more seconds, she realized he wasn't going to say more. Finally, they walked toward his truck; the vehicle was already running with white smoke puffing from the exhaust pipe. Gold hesitated at the driver's side as she watched Troy carefully stand, fold his chair, then slide into the driver's seat. She hopped in the passenger side, while he settled his chair in the back.

She took a little longer with her seatbelt than necessary. She liked him pulling her hair and pinching her nipple. The tingles from her scalp and breast were still vibrating through her system. And she could scent the earthy smell of her arousal.

"Yes," she murmured.

Troy pushed the button for drive and pulled away from the parking space. He nearly missed what she said and had to replay the words in his head. When he did, a slow smile split his face. "I can definitely work with that."

Chapter Three

"This isn't the way to my home," Gold protested, as he turned left onto Jackson Road.

"You never told me where you live." Troy zipped up the dark road until he reached a street before a lighted sign announced Scio Farms. He made the left onto a two-lane road, switched to high beams, and then stopped in the drive of a farmhouse. He entered the oversize garage. The door lowered noiselessly as he parked the car and turned in his seat.

"I'd like to explore more of what we did in the parking lot."

"Maybe this isn't a good idea," she began, as she reached for the door handle.

"What are you afraid of, Gold?" He took her left hand in his. "We have chemistry between us." He drew circles on the back of her hand with his thumb. Her skin was so soft compared to his rough, calloused hands. No matter what moisturizers he used, his hands were always tough, and he would forever have callouses, not only from his wheelchair but from weights at the gym. But her skin? He could lose himself in the texture, the silky smoothness. He brought her hand to his mouth and licked the knuckle before he grazed his teeth over the bone.

Her quick inhale told him he was doing something right. He turned her hand over, gently biting the fleshy part of the heel. From the corner of his eyes, he watched her lashes flutter as she crossed her legs.

She was so responsive to his touch, and he was only kissing her hand. How would she react if he had her entire body to explore?

Some catchy tune played on a xylophone split the sexually charged air. Gold scrambled in her pocket for her phone. "It's my dad."

Reluctantly, Troy released her hand.

"Dad? Is everything all right?"

Troy studied her a moment. So close. He'd been so close to getting her inside his home and maybe naked. As unobtrusively as possible, he shifted his erection to a more comfortable position. All sorts of images flooded his mind. Gold on her knees, blindfolded, waiting for him to touch her. Gold spread across his lap, her bottom red from a spanking.

"No, I'm with a friend. We had dinner," he heard her say.

He had to stop thinking such lurid thoughts or he'd never get out of his truck. He wanted to be more than friends with Gold.

"Can it wait?" A plaintive note clung to her voice. "I'm a little busy."

Hope surged anew. Could she possibly be putting her dad's request on hold in order to spend more time with him? As if to curry more favor, he caressed her thigh.

"I'll call you when I get home," she promised. She locked gazes with Troy. "Or better yet, when I get up in the morning."

His house was not what Gold expected. She unwound her scarf and stuffed it in the sleeve of her coat, resting the garment over the back of a nearby chair. The colors on the walls were warm peaches, golds, and ambers: it worked well with the dark wood floors. She moved forward in her socked feet. The furniture was sturdy, expensive, and well-made. She trailed her fingers along the back of a leather sofa. So smooth and supple.

What drew her attention most was the fireplace. The brick hearth was elevated, and there was enough of a ledge to where she could safely sit in front of the flames, if she so chose.

"I could start a fire if you like," he offered.

"I would."

The pleasure stole through him at her admission, and he realized he wanted to please her, from the moment he'd seen her. Well, maybe not the very moment, but once he noticed how hard she worked during the workouts.

There were a handful of participants who actually took the workouts seriously, and Gold was one of them. When some of the others wanted to quit, or did quit, because a particular exercise was too hard or their muscles hurt, Gold pushed through and asked for more.

He moved the chain curtain aside. Kindling and firewood was already stacked; he only had to set a match to the stack. The wood caught and he pulled the curtain back in place.

"Would you like something to drink?" He wheeled to face her.

She settled on the edge of the hearth, and they were nearly eye to eye. Firelight caught her pretty features accentuating her dark eyes, now wide with care and wonder. She stared at the flames transfixed.

He cupped her cheek, leaned forward, and captured her mouth.

This time his kiss was soft, seductive, coaxing. He wanted to show her he had a softer side.

She tasted so sweet; he pulled her closer, deepening the kiss until she grasped his biceps. The fired warmed his skin, and he shifted to bring her into his lap.

"Oh," she murmured as he cradled her.

"Problem?" he queried between kisses.

"Not really."

Troy stared into her eyes, slipping his fingers beneath her shirt. There was all that soft skin again, begging for his exploration. He skimmed eager fingers over her taut abs, another sign she'd taken her workouts seriously. Everywhere he touched was smooth and toned. He had a need to see her without her clothes.

"Take them off," he ordered huskily.

On shaky legs, Gold stood. She stared at Troy for a moment, a tiny bit of apprehension tickled her bloodstream and heightened her desire. She hesitated as she tried to remember the condition of her underwear. The lacy bra she wore was fairly new and one of her faves, but did her panties have any rips or tears in them? She couldn't remember. At least she didn't think there were any holes in her panties. If there were ... she bowed her head as she fumbled with the buttons on her shirt.

"What's that look for?" Troy demanded.

Heat crept into her cheeks, and she paused with her arms crisscrossed at her middle. Did she tell him the truth? If there were holes, he'd see them for himself. Or she could flip the script and tell him no. To save herself more embarrassment?

"Gold?"

She finished unbuttoning her shirt, slid it off her shoulders. "Hmm?"

"I asked you a question."

"I'm deciding how to answer," she replied truthfully. With trembling fingers, she folded her shirt, then set it on the small table.

"The truth is always best," he said, a hint of humor in his voice.

She unfastened her slacks. "I think my panties may have a hole in them," she mumbled.

He rolled closer, reached up and, with his fingers beneath her chin, tilted her head until their gazes met. "What was that?"

"I think the lace is ripped in my underwear," she responded defensively. "And I was trying to figure out if I should put a stop to this to save face or just go with it."

He lifted slightly in his chair and placed the gentlest kiss, just a flutter of butterfly wings against her lips. "Thank you for telling me. I can see how difficult it was for you." He withdrew, and her hands slipped from her pants.

The material puddled at her feet. She pressed fingertips to her lips, as if to hold the kiss in place. The praise, accompanied by the caress, moved her more than she thought possible. Was she so starved for a man's affection that a few pretty words and an amazing kiss turned her brain to mush?

"Turn around."

She complied before she realized what she was doing. The heat from the fire kept her warm as she did a slow pirouette, careful not to trip over her pants.

"No holes," he announced.

Relief flooded through her, and she released a little giggle. "Well, small mercies."

He waved a hand toward her slacks. "Are you going to fold those?"

When she bent to retrieve the garment, he swatted her bottom.

"Hey!" She shot upright, clutching her pants to her breasts with one hand and the other hand rubbing the stinging spot on her buttocks. The simple contact, though unexpected, had a sliver of heat sidling through her veins. She wanted him to do it again.

"You liked that," he observed.

Slowly, she nodded. "I did."

With practiced ease, he swung his wheelchair around. "Good. Follow me."

A little bewildered, Gold hurried after him. Her socked feet made no noise on the wood. She still clutched her slacks in her hand and quickly folded them as she went. He paused at a door at the end of the hall. Every other door was open. She could see into a bedroom turned office, a bathroom, and what was obviously his room. Troy took a key from his pocket and fit it in the lock.

She raised a brow. "A locked room?"

He grinned. "You'll love it."

She cast him a skeptical look as she stepped past him. He reached in and flicked on a light. Gold blinked in the sudden brightness. Padded, leather benches in varying heights and lengths dotted the room. On one wall, various implements from leather paddles and straps all the way to a large hook thing, which reminded her of an old-fashioned carpet beater. Floggers, in leather, rope, or even softer materials hung next to the assortment of paddles. She lifted a hand to touch one and stopped.

"May I?" she glanced over her shoulder. This was something she'd always wanted to try, but never had the opportunity.

"I can even test it out on you," he offered.

Gold removed the flogger and ran her fingers over the tails, which were made of velvet. Absently, she set her folded pants on a nearby bench, replaced the flogger, and picked up a square leather paddle. It wasn't so much a paddle as a strap. She ran it through her fingers; the texture was supple. It reminded her of a strap a barber would use to hone a straight razor.

Troy plucked the strap from her hand and placed it on his lap before handing her a thick oak paddle.

The texture was smooth and cool. When she turned it over, she was surprised to find the other side held texture, coarse like that of a basketball. "Very cool."

"Indeed." He wheeled a few feet away, plucking one implement or another from their hooks. He settled these on a table near a waist high bench. Turning, he placed her hand on his shoulder and led her to the bench.

"Place your hands on the bench and lean forward a bit," he instructed.

Gold complied. "I've never done this before," she admitted.

"We'll go off the traffic light system," he explained. "Red means stop. Yellow slow down and green means go. I'm rather heavy-handed, so we'll go slow and get a feel for what you can tolerate."

"I usually have a high tolerance for pain."

"We'll see." He traced the skin above the waistband of her panties. A tingle of anticipation raced through her. "I love your skin." He placed a kiss at the small of her back. "So soft and tempting."

She curled her fingers into the supple leather. There was something decadent about the way he touched her; there was reverence in his touch and something else. He cupped her buttocks; the rasps of his palms sparked a longing for him to skim his fingers across her very center. He drew her panties up, tightening them against her skin, and he spanked one cheek and then the other.

"How is that?"

"Mmm. You could go a little harder."

Troy smiled and spanked her again. She didn't utter a moan or a whimper. He studied her face and body for any type of distress. A fine sheen of sweat formed at her hairline, but other than that, she seemed to enjoy what he was doing. He shifted to grab the leather strap. He brought the leather down on her lace-covered bottom. She jerked but didn't utter a sound. Two quick successive smacks. How hard would he have to strike her in order to get a verbal response? Two more and a little harder. She winced, lifting her left foot just a bit. A smile curved his lips.

"Harder," she breathed, fingers flexed on the bench.

After each slap of the leather strap, Gold accessed the sensations rolling through her body. The sting of the strap bloomed until it burned through nerve endings, pooled in the crotch of her panties, and flowed outward.

For once, her mind was quiet, focusing on the pain/pleasure Troy demanded from her body. Each strike, each new implement against her skin, allowed her to sink deeper into sensation. Gentle fingers tugged at her panties. Slowly, he drew the lace down her hips. Cool air skittered across her heated flesh; the feeling only intensified as he dragged his fingernails over the sensitive flesh. He followed this with his lips. She couldn't stop the moan of pleasure from easing past her lips.

At her response, he applied an open palm to each cheek. Liquid desire slicked her inner thighs. Carefully, Troy stood. He pressed against Gold, reaching around to cup her breasts. They fit neatly in the palms of his hands. He brushed a kiss along the curve of her shoulder as he squeezed her nipples.

She grinded against his erection. He nipped the curve of her shoulder. "I didn't tell you to move."

She froze. Uh oh. What was he going to do now?

He stepped away, to again sit in his chair. Shivering at the loss of his body heat. She wanted him back, feeling his hard body pressed against hers, his hands once again stroking her skin or something instead of this terrible sense of loss. She hung her head.

She nearly jumped from her skin when something soft and velvety struck her back, then slid over her buttocks. This was more sensual than painful, and she wasn't sure if she liked it, but it did have her wanting more. She yearned for a little harder. Impatient, she shifted from one foot to the other.

Chuckling softly, he reached up to her bra. He slipped one strap down her arm and then the other, before he unfastened each of the three hooks on the back. The bra fell to the bench, but she didn't move.

"Good girl," he praised. A sharp sting spread along her shoulders, with the air becoming cool as he flicked his wrist again. Different flogger, more pain. He mixed them until she was never sure if she would get sting or softness.

In somewhat of a daze, he led her from the room into his bedroom. There he peeled back the comforter. "Lie down on your stomach."

Gold settled into sheets and inhaled deeply. She was surrounded by his scent and settled more fully into the mattress, pillowing her head on her arms.

The bed dipped beside her. A moment later something cool and fragrant, like coconuts, along with strong, calloused hands smoothed over the welts on her back and buttocks. He traced one line.

"Such beautiful skin," he murmured. Once he finished massaging the oil into her skin, he covered her with the blanket and laid beside her.

Gold snuggled close, and he held her a little tighter. "That was amazing."

"You are amazing," he said. "I've never had anyone take what you did."

She chuckled. "I wasn't sure if I would like pain like that. For the first time in a long time, my mind is quiet."

He stroked her hair from her face before caressing her ear. She had such beautiful ears. He kissed the delicate shell.

"I feel like I'm floating."

He did too. For the time they were in his playroom, he hadn't felt any pain. Even now, with her in his arms, his body relaxed enough that there was no pain.

"Stay the night."

"I don't think I could move," she confessed. "Could we do this again?"

"Absolutely."

Chapter Four

"She's going to love this," Gold exclaimed, as she carefully sat in one of the cushioned chairs. Her bottom was deliciously sore, and all she could think about was the time she'd spent with Troy last night. Now she was having a hard time focusing on the task before her, selecting a cake design for Geneva's surprise baby shower.

Geneva's husband, Jethro, picked up a sketch and held it close to his face before turning his attention to one of three small models.

"These are magnificent," Jethro praised. He set down the sketch and picked up one of the small-tiered cakes. They were no higher than a foot, but were 3-D replicas of what was on the paper. "These are amazing."

"Thanks," Penelope said. "I make the models, and Avery or one of the girls does the sketch. That way any one of us can replicate the design." Penelope brushed her hand along the desk until she touched one of the models. "And changes can be made to the design." She carefully removed the tiny butterfly and placed it on another spot to demonstrate before returning it to its original position.

"I've never actually seen your creations," Jethro began. "Or rather never paid attention to them. Although I've always enjoyed the final product."

They laughed.

Jethro ran his fingers over each model. All had a baby cradled as its topper, but each design was different. One held butterflies and storks. Another was decorated in tiny blue and pink flowers, and the final one held things like baby blocks, diaper pins, and what looked to be a stack of diapers. All of them seemed to incorporate tiny footsteps and baby booties.

"We don't know the sex," Jethro said.

"She mentioned you both wanted to be surprised," Gold stated.

Jethro tapped the third sketch, the one that held more baby items. He pushed the corresponding model toward Penelope. "I think this is the winner. She'll get a kick out of all the baby stuff."

Gold sat back and listened to the two of them hammer out the details of the cake from the flavor of the layers to the filling and type of buttercream. She had no idea how much went into a simple cake.

Her phone vibrated her hip. Startled, she jumped upright and winced, having forgotten about her butt. "Excuse me. I need to take this." She pulled out her phone as she left the room. The number displayed was one she didn't recognize, so she decided to answer with her professional title, especially if it was a patient. "Dr. Falls, how may I help you?"

"Dr. Falls, is it?"

Warmth spread through at hearing the gruff voice. "Troy. How lovely to hear from you." She leaned against the wall, far away from the main part of the shop and farthest from the room she'd exited. From her vantage point, she could watch the comings and goings of the patrons without being seen or overheard.

"I'm calling to check on you. Make sure you're not experiencing any sub-drop."

Gold smiled. She was familiar with the term. So far she was good, though aware the phenomena, of adrenaline or endorphins—those feel good emotions especially after such an intense scene like they had last night could cause her mood to plummet—could strike anywhere from a few hours to a few days after play. "So far so good. But if I experience any negative emotions, I will let you know," she promised.

"Good. I don't want you to be alone if it can be helped."

"And how are you doing?"

"Between classes at the moment. We could get a bite to eat after class tonight. And we could talk some more."

"I'd like that."

"And how is that sweet ass of yours?"

Now she grinned. "Sore, as you well know."

She could hear his smile through the line. "Soon, we'll have it so you won't be able to sit for a week." With that husky promise, he ended the call.

Slowly, Gold lowered her phone. What a delicious promise.

❧

"And go!" Robin, one of the trainers, called out.

Gold pulled the short handle of the rower back until it met her chest, the padded seat glided backward, while her feet, anchored into the Velcro straps, kept her from sliding off the machine. She allowed the cable to pull her forward in a controlled motion. She brushed sweat from her brow on the shoulder of her shirt. They were barely halfway through a cardio-heavy circuit.

August was on her left, while Jason and Samson worked the stationary bikes to her right. On the far right of the room, Troy was harassing two other people who'd joined the class in the last few weeks.

Every now and then, she would sneak glances at him. He looked good in the black tee with some logo painted on the front and a bandana to hold back his locks, while black sweatpants and sneakers completed his ensemble.

"And rest."

Gold slowed her pace but did not stop.

"I've lost another thirty pounds since starting this class," August stated. "And the best part is I've got some serious muscles and toned butt."

Gold laughed. "Congrats! And same on the muscle tone. Didn't think I'd ever achieve my goal either."

"If you're laughing, you're not sweating," Troy called.

"Mind your business," August called good-naturedly.

"And go!" Robin called out.

Gold increased her pace. Her shoulders burned with the effort, so she moved her hands to the ends of the bar. With the wider hand placement, this would access a different part of the muscle.

"He loves the trash talk," Gold panted.

August giggled. "I know, keeps him on his toes."

For the next few seconds, Gold concentrated on getting through the cycle. After this, there would be squats and then back to a cardio machine. Or maybe she would push one of the sleds up and down the floor.

"I'm having a few friends over this weekend. I'd like you to be there if you can make it," August stated.

"Sure. Should I bring anything?"

"Jason and GG are cooking, and they always make way more food than any three people can eat."

"Heard that, Sol," Jason piped up.

"Well, it's true."

Jason's familiar "heh heh" rolled through the gym. Gold grinned. The man had the best laugh in the world. Every time she heard it, she wanted to join in.

"Time to change," Robin announced.

Gold slowly let the machine pull her forward and released the handle. Wiping her face with a hand towel, she extracted her feet from the straps, then stood. "August? Do you need an elbow?" she asked.

"Thanks."

Gold waited until August laid a light hand on her elbow before they traversed the gym to a row of weight benches. There were five of them. Beyond them and nearly to the front door was a rack of weights and kettle bells. A collection of stretch bands also hung above the weights.

"The bench is three steps to your left," Gold informed. She waited while August slid a foot until she touched the bench in question, then reached down a hand to feel for the seat. Once August was seated, Gold took the next bench over.

"Here are some waters, ladies." Robin handed each a water. "Do you know what weights you want?"

"Twenty pounds, at least," Troy sang out.

Gold glared in his general direction. "Seriously?" She swigged her water.

August clapped her hands. "Bring it!" she challenged.

"Don't encourage him," Gold murmured. She accepted the kettle bell from Robin, then glanced at the white numbers stenciled on the front: 15. Gold chuckled.

Troy wheeled over, plucked the weight from her hand, and wheeled away. "I don't think so." He returned a moment later with a 25-lb. weight. "And make sure you count."

Biting back a grin, Gold gripped the handle, flipped the weight upside down and worked through the sets of squats.

⌒

A wave of admiration rolled through Troy as he watched Gold knock out the three sets of squats, then push and pull the weighted sled up and down the gym floor. Now she was sweating on the bike. Her glasses were perched precariously on the end of her nose while sweat freely flowed down her face. It was the same look of concentration she wore on her face the night before, while he applied different implements to her bare flesh.

What an amazing time they had. Not only had she taken the best he had to offer, she'd asked for more. For her first time he didn't want to overwhelm her, but he did want to see how far he could stretch her boundaries.

He piled a few loose weights in his lap, intending to return them to the storage rack. Those back in their respective slots, he wheeled toward Jason and Samson. Both men were doing chest presses. Samson's form was a little off.

"Yo Stx," Troy began. "Why you slacking over here? Act like you hugging a grizzly bear." He touched the man's elbow and with his other widened the arms.

"Has anybody ever hit you with a weight?" Samson asked good-naturedly.

"No."

"Well, there's always a first."

Jason burst out laughing.

"What's so funny, sandbag?" Troy demanded. "I don't hear none of y'all counting."

Neither man spoke, only grunted. "Six. Twelve. Thirty-five," he intoned loudly.

"You know he only does that to throw us off," Samson commented.

Jason laughed his memorable laugh. "That was the last one."

Troy scanned the gym, already looking for his next victim to harass. Once again, his gaze settled on Gold. Now she was on a mat, legs together in the air, while she curled her torso and tried to touch her toes. She made the move seem so effortless. He remembered when she only had the strength to do three, had to stop before continuing. Now she knocked out the ab work like nothing.

He had her naked body next to his all night long. No matter how much he wanted to be inside her, there was always the chance he wouldn't be able to satisfy her. Would she think of him as less than a man? Or, worse, laugh at him for not being able to consistently perform?

He had to make an adjustment after the accident in his life as his disease progressed. Lately, the medication he was on helped the flare-ups, but at a cost. Most women were turned off if he couldn't have sex, so BDSM became his outlet.

He studied Gold as she slowed her pace, then wiped her face with the hand towel she kept at her waist. So beautiful, and he could so easily fall for her. He swiveled his chair turning his attention back to the men. They were on the rower. "C'mon, sandbag! You're letting the women beat you."

Chapter Five

T roy set the table, then settled a trivet between the place settings. The veggie lasagna was due out of the oven any moment. He'd long since showered and dressed in comfortable clothes, in this case jeans and a sweatshirt. He'd left his front door unlocked so Gold could just walk in and had just removed the salad from the refrigerator when the phone rang.

"Yes," he answered when picking up the phone.

"You have something I want," a menacing voice began. "I want it back."

"Who is this?" Troy demanded. A swirl of cold air blew through the house as the front door opened.

"You've been warned."

"Something smells great," Gold called out cheerily.

Frowning, Troy hung up the phone.

"Is something wrong?" Gold hovered in the doorway, watching him with anxious eyes.

"Strange phone call," he answered. He stood, walked the few steps to her, and kissed her.

She clutched his waist, giving herself over to his heated kiss. He nipped her bottom lip before deepening the kiss.

She opened for him, as if they'd done this every day of their lives. Slowly, he walked her backward until he sat in one of the kitchen chairs. She followed him down, straddling his lap.

The bulge in his jeans settled at the heat of her core. She grinded against him in response.

This man made her forget all rational thought. When they were alone together, there was only the way he made her feel.

"What are you doing to me?" she murmured against his lips. "All I can do is think about the way your hands feel on my skin or the way your lips taste."

He shifted, grabbing a handful of her sore ass. She winced. He smiled. "You like that."

"I do."

"How does the rest of you feel?"

"Pretty good considering the workout you put us through today."

Her fingers went to the waist band of his jeans. "There are parts of your body I still want to taste."

He tried to shackle her wrists, but she was already sliding to the floor, unfastening his jeans and freeing him from the material with practiced ease. His cock sprang forth long, thick, and hard.

When she flicked an experimental tongue across the broad head of his penis, he closed his eyes in pleasure. He nearly forgot to breathe when she sucked him into her mouth, swirled her tongue along the slit, and sucked him deep. Troy forgot all about the constant pain, his weakening joints, and how his immune system attacked his body, concentrating instead on the pleasure coursing through his veins.

She even used the right number of teeth just the way he liked. He fisted a hand into her hair, holding her in place as he flexed his hips. She hummed around him, the sound vibrating through him, and he cursed the fact that he wasn't naked.

"Woman, you're killing me."

She chuckled and sucked harder. And then the unthinkable happened. He was enjoying this fantastic blowjob, and now he was flaccid.

"Fuck!"

As if sensing his frustration, Gold kissed his flaccid member, then wedged herself between his legs until she could kiss his lips.

"Relax," she said.

"But I can't satisfy you," he told her, bitterness in his voice. "That's why I wanted to talk to you tonight. There will be times I'm rock hard and the next limp."

She stroked a hand over his cheek while she pressed her other palm to his heart. "It's a good thing you got all that gruff personality going for you."

He stared into her eyes. There was no condemnation. No judgement, just a willingness to work with him, please him, and be pleased. Even now, lust simmered in her irises, lust for him and something else.

"Gold."

"I saw your playroom, Troy. Are you telling me you don't have dildos, vibrators, and butt plugs in there?" A mischievous smile flirted at her mouth. "Or should I look for some glow-in-the-dark cock rings?" While she spoke, she stroked him from tip to balls. "You had me naked in your bed last night, and you satisfied a need I didn't even know I had."

He grew hard in her hand. "Are you saying you don't know how to use your mouth for anything other than trash talk?"

In one fluid motion, he shifted her over his knee. She squealed as he brought his hand down on her bottom. She pressed her palms into the floor as her toes sought purchase on the tile. She squirmed on his lap, doing her best not to giggle.

"Is that your answer for everything? Spank me until I submit?"

"You'd submit even if I didn't spank you."

"True, but this only incentivizes me."

He brought his hand down on her bottom, and she squirmed some more. She hadn't made him feel bad for losing his erection. He smoothed his hand over her warming backside, pleased to see she wore a skirt as he'd asked. He lifted the hem to find she had on no panties.

"You do follow directions." He stroked her petal soft skin. Even with the swelling from their earlier play, her skin was still soft.

He allowed his hand to dip lower, following the seam of her core, until he found damp heat. She was so wet for him. One lone finger eased into her tightness, and he was rewarded with a throaty moan. He closed his eyes savoring the sound, the sensation.

He slid in and out, pulling more of her spicy heat and slicking it around her folds.

He wanted to taste her.

"Go to the playroom." He helped her to an upright position.

Nodding, she left the kitchen. Gold listened as Troy banged around the kitchen behind her. Every movement glided the material of her clothing against her over sensitized skin. She had to resist the temptation to lift her skirt and plunge her fingers in her pussy just to stop the incessant ache. One hand cupped and pinched her nipple before she realized what she was doing. How could he have her so switched on? Probably because it was new. She stopped at the closed door and tried the knob. It was locked, so she stood there and breathed.

She never would've walked out of the house in the dead of winter in a skirt and no panties. But she had. She was even standing here with her head resting on a door, waiting for Troy to inflict more pain on her body. And she found it exciting.

She who listened and guided everyday people through simple life changes to extraordinary traumatic events questioned her willingness to abandon what was considered normal for the unusual.

"Did I not leave it unlocked?"

She kept her face to the door. "It's locked."

Keys rattled as he reached past her to open the door. "Strip, then enter."

She smiled, loving how gruff his voice turned. "I'm beginning to think all you want to do is see me naked." She shed her clothes, folding each garment as she went. When she entered the room, she set them on the small table just inside the door.

Candles illuminated the space, casting long shadows and giving the room an intimate glow. She noticed not all the candles were real. Several of the larger pillar ones were battery operated, while several of the taper candles had flickering flames. These were set in protective candleholders.

"Where would you like me?" She met his gaze, surprised at the hunger in the chocolate depths.

He gave a faint nod toward a narrow bed, no bigger than a standard massage table. This one had a few modifications. D-rings were bolted at the head and foot of the table. She could see the restraints fastened in place.

Her pulse quickened at the thought of being bound. She fingered the padded leather cuffs before sliding onto the mattress. The sheet was silky soft, and she ran her fingers back and forth, reveling its luxury.

"Did you come up with a safe word?" He trailed his fingers along her flesh, relishing the slight tremor.

"I did."

He wheeled to the head of the bed, carefully removed her glasses, then placed them in his shirt pocket.

Gold blinked. Without her glasses, there were only distinct blobs and blurs. "Don't lose those now. I'm totally blind without my glasses."

"Trust me to take care of you, love," Troy muttered, leaning over to kiss her. "I have every intention of meeting your needs." He squeezed her breasts, rolling her nipples between his fingers. "Raise your arms above your head and hold your hands together."

"Like this?" She crossed her wrists above her head.

"Yes." He quickly shackled her wrists. Once they were fastened, he placed a pinky finger between the cuff and her wrists. "How does that feel? Too tight?"

"Feels fine."

He then strapped each of her ankles. She could bend her knees, but she wasn't going anywhere. Here she was splayed for his scrutiny, and part of her felt exposed but also powerful. He ran a finger down her core, circling her clit until her hips bucked.

"And as you reminded me, there's more than just my dick to satisfy you."

"Did I say that?" she asked breathlessly.

He pinched her clit, pleased when she hissed a breath. "You did."

"Sometimes I have a smart mouth," she admitted.

He inserted a finger while he played with her little pearl. "You do, but you've got enough to cash that check your mouth likes to write." He brought his fingers to his mouth, licking her essence.

Gold trembled. His fingers were deft and sure as he stroked her dewy folds. She bit her lip as a slow fire built in her bloodstream. She shifted on the bed, trying to bring her body in the right contact to his fingers. Every time she tried to get the right pressure, he would shift his movements.

He kissed her ankle, slowly working his way up one leg and down the other. He paused at the juncture of her thighs. The long, slow rasp of his tongue dried the saliva in her mouth. She clenched the edge of the bed, as her hips rose to meet the most intimate kiss.

"Oh God." Fascinated, Troy licked again, hoping he'd get the same response. He was rewarded with more of her sweet, hot cream. She tried to close her legs and shift away, but he was having none of that. He wedged his shoulders between her thighs, shortening the ankle straps to keep her open to him and clamped his hand on her hips.

He teased her clit, coaxing it out until it hardened. He speared his tongue deep, lapping at every drop of heat she secreted.

She whimpered, trying to place her pussy to his mouth in the spot she wanted, and gasped. He was so strong, she could barely move. And the fire he'd kindled was so hot, it threatened to burn her entirely. Only he could quench the flames and all he was doing was stroking it higher and hotter.

"Oh please," she begged. She was going to combust if he didn't let her have an orgasm.

"Please what?" he prompted. He reached up to circle her nipple.

Her mind blanked. What was she supposed to say? Something cool whispered against her skin a moment before a sharp bite of pain bloomed, then spread into fiery pleasure.

"Ah. You like nipple clamps." He smiled.

She heard the approval in his voice. "Yes."

The other clamp fastened to her other breast, and she sank into the sensation. Intense pleasure zipped from nipples to clit and back again.

Troy tugged the chain, studying Gold for every reaction. The way she bit her lip or how her fingers curled, even the way her hips moved in an effort to seek relief from the pleasure he was giving her, she was so open to him. And now he had an idea.

He dipped his finger again in her heat, then spread the goodness to her little pucker. She only moaned, allowing her knees to fall wider. Smiling, he opened a small drawer beneath the bed and removed a jar of coconut oil.

He dipped a finger, removed a generous amount, and applied it to her anus, working it in and around the opening, going slow as not to hurt her.

Gold tensed at the sudden pressure. It felt good, but also painful.

"Relax," he soothed. He caressed her legs, leaned forward, and licked her pussy. When he felt the tension ease from her body, he pushed his finger little deeper. She was tight. So very tight, and he knew she'd never had any back-door pleasure. He moved his finger in and out, keeping the movement slow and deliberate. When her hips moved in time with his strokes, he eased in another finger.

Tension coiled tight in the pit of Gold's belly. Every sense she had focused on the pleasure: nipples, ass, and pussy. How had she never experienced sensations such as this before? When Troy removed his fingers from her butt, she almost cried out at the loss.

He chuckled. "Don't worry, I'll fill it with some-thing else."

Pressure built again, and she wasn't sure she could take what he was pressing into her tightness. As soon as she thought she couldn't handle anymore, the pressure stopped, then built again.

"Anal beads," he answered her unspoken question.

The second and third bead left her panting. Each one seemed bigger than the last.

"Can you take one more for me?" he queried softly.

For him, she would try. "Yes."

He pushed the fourth and final bead inside, and all she could do was pant.

"You hold that there while I wash my hands."

Gold had no choice, being bound, clamped, and spread for his pleasure. Every time she moved, no matter how small, the movement sensation swamped her body. Her nipples were on fire, her pussy throbbed, and the pressure in her ass begged for release. She wanted, no needed, some relief.

At the sudden vibration, she nearly came off the bed. "Bastard." The beads vibrated and gyrated, adding to the sensations already overwhelming her senses.

Laughter floated over the running water.

"My. My. You have such bad vocabulary," he admonished.

He was worried about her bad vocabulary when she could no longer form a coherent thought.

He returned, running his hands over sensitized flesh. She moaned, arching toward his touch. Where his hands moved, his lips and tongue followed. Every now and then, he tugged at the chain strumming band, plucking moans, gasps, and whimpers as easily as playing a guitar.

Everything swirled, coalescing until she poised on a razor thin edge of pleasure/pain. She was so close to her climax. Yet every time she reached the point, he'd back off, allowing the surge to recede, then building it again.

Gold clenched her fists, sweat running into her brow. "I can't. It's too much."

Hands that were rough before were so infinitely gentle she could've sobbed. The touch was too light when all she wanted, no needed, was relief from the fire consuming her.

"You are mine," he whispered against her lips.

"I'm yours," she repeated.

"This body is mine to do with as I please."

"Yes," she readily agreed.

He moved between her legs again, kissed the glistening folds.

She quivered beneath him. He grasped her hips, latched onto her clit, and sucked.

Gold tensed, her entire being center on Troy's hot mouth feasting at her womanly buffet. Anal beads, nipple clamps, and now his tongue and lips tormenting her even more⊠it was too much. She shattered. And he did not stop. He reached up and snatched off the clamps. Another orgasm crashed over and through her. She screamed and still, he did not stop. He continued eating and licking her body, bowing to the ebbs and flow of his hands and mouth. At the third climax, she could only whimper, her body drenched in sweat as he slowly eased the assault on her clit. He placed a soft, little kiss, as he slowly pulled each bead from her anus.

This brought fresh waves of aftershocks and pleasure so strong, tears leaked from her eyes. She was combusting. The flames he'd built roared from the very marrow of her bones and burned through her flesh, singeing every nerve, muscle, and cell. She laid there as little shudders were breaking over and through her.

She didn't even realize she'd been released until he gathered her in his arms and settled her in his lap. She curled against him as he wheeled them into his bedroom.

On unsteady limbs, she crawled into the big bed and collapsed on her stomach. Troy returned with a warm, wet cloth and cleaned her up. She shuddered.

He grinned. It would be so easy to send her into another orgasm, as her body was primed and ready for more. He quickly shed his clothes and crawled in beside her.

She barely moved as he settled her in his arms.

"You did so well," he praised.

She brushed a kiss long his chest. "I can't move." Laughter rumbled beneath her cheek.

"You can move." He shifted until she sprawled atop him. He shifted her until his erection met the entrance of her heat. Slowly she slid over him, impaling herself on his hardness. The hard length scraped over already sensitive nerves. She groaned as he stretched and filled her, another climax building as he thrust upward.

"Ride me."

She did.

Chapter Six

They ate lukewarm lasagna and salad on a blanket in front of the fireplace. Gold adjusted the hem of the borrowed tee shirt she wore. She brought part of the garment to her nose, inhaling Troy's crisp, clean scent.

"I like the way you look in my shirt," he told her.

"I like being in your shirt."

He reached over and rubbed a hand over her calf. "Are you okay?"

"Body is sore in all the right places," she assured him.

He cleared the last of the food from his plate, then set the empty dish on a nearby coffee table. "What are you thinking?"

"How do you know I'm thinking?"

"You have a tendency to bite your lip when thinking."

She touched her mouth, like she was doing right now. For a moment, she gazed into the fire. "Did you mean what you said, or was it in the heat of the moment?"

"When I said what?"

She shifted until she stared straight into his eyes. "That I'm yours."

Grasping her ankle, Troy pulled her closer. Gold had just enough time to set her plate aside before he blanketed her body. He framed her face. "You are mine." He closed his lips over her nipple and sucked hard.

Gold cradled the back of his head, arching into him. A tiny sigh eased past her lips.

"You make me feel whole." He suckled her other breast until twin wet spots marred the fabric. "I could play your body all day every day and never tire of it."

She squeezed her eyes closed as a single tear leaked out. "We hardly know one another."

"We've known each other for months now, Gold. We haven't spent enough time alone to truly pursue one another," he corrected. He leaned on one elbow, studying her face. "I wanted you from the moment I first saw you."

She reached up and ran her fingers through his locs.

He kissed the inside of her wrist.

"Why BDSM?" She raised slightly, drawing her glass of water closer.

"At first, simple curiosity. After the accident and injury to my spine, coupled with my lupus flares, I learned more and kept BDSM as an outlet. I could assuage some of my sexual need by bringing others pleasure." He lifted her plate from where it rested, forked up a bit of the lasagna, and held it to her lips.

There was an intimacy to having him feed her. And it struck her; he was taking care of her. Where most thought in terms of having a man provide a home and comfort, he was seeing that not just her mind and spirit were fed, but her body as well.

"I've got to admit my emotions are all over the place right now." She blinked back the burn of tears.

"Eat." He held up another forkful. "And I have a bit of chocolate for dessert."

She chewed the last bite, swallowed, then sipped more water. "Thanks."

"I've pushed you hard the last couple of days."

She cupped his cheek. "I've enjoyed every moment."

He sat up and stacked her empty plate on his.

"Is there a time when you're not in pain?"

Surprise clouded his irises. "How did you know?"

"Your voice changes," she answered. "It's a little thing, but you get a little gravellier."

"You're the first person to point that out."

"I'm also a trained therapist," she reminded him.

"Yes. The extremely talented, intelligent, and beautiful Dr. Falls."

Laughing, she poked him in the chest. "And don't you forget it."

"Stay the night again?"

"Yes."

Troy was up early, despite the late night. He stifled a yawn. The gym was quiet this time of the morning. No music, but the faint scent of rubber and sweat clung to the air. He smiled. The hard work and determination were the best smells in the world. This was his gym, and he was proud of what he'd accomplished. An adaptive trainer, giving those with physical challenges and other disabilities a chance to exercise in a safe environment. There were weighted plates for those who couldn't grasp a traditional dumbbell. Any exercise done a traditional way could be modified for someone in a wheelchair, walker, with prosthetic limbs. If the person was willing to put in the work, Troy was willing to work the person.

He sat on one of the recumbent bikes, fastened his feet to the pedals, and worked the handles. He winced. The joints were still a little stiff, but the exercise would help. The exercise always helped with muscle tone and keeping him in shape. Once his muscles were warmed, he moved to bench presses. He pumped iron until a fine sheen of sweat coated his brow. Replacing the heavy weight in the safety rack with a metallic clang before reaching for his water bottle.

He'd met Gold here. For the first time in a long time, he felt like he could be himself with her. He didn't have to pretend he wasn't in pain or make excuses for a failing erection. She accepted everything.

Never had a woman just accepted him and what he offered. Being with her these last few days made him realize he wanted to have her for the rest of their lives. He wanted to take care of her, see to her needs and wants. Allow her a chance to be her sensual self without judgment. He would love waking up to her in his bed and having her beside him at night. It had been a long time since he let a woman in his space as he had Gold.

Metal tapping on glass drew his attention. Troy squinted toward the front door. Here was his first client. Time to get to work.

Gold ducked her chin, as a gust of arctic air blew. The sun shone bright in the pale blue sky. Heavy white clouds promised snow later. She hurried up the sidewalk to the co-op on the corner. She paused, changed her mind, and continued across the street to the Kerrytown market.

She stepped a little too hard off the curb and winced. Her body was still sore from a combination of her workouts, play, and lovemaking with Troy.

A slow smile creased her lips. The man was pretty inventive, and he thought he couldn't satisfy her? A happy giggle filled the air, until she clamped a hand over her mouth. She had to resist the urge to skip, she was so happy.

Once inside the building, Gold breathed a sigh of relief. Warmth enveloped her, and she loosened her scarf. Maybe some sort of soup and a sandwich would be good. She perused the blackboard with the lunch specials. Oo, chicken pot pie was on the menu; now that would be awesome. From previous visits, she knew the restaurant made individual pies filled with chunks of chicken, veggies, and a creamy gravy; the best part was the super flaky crust.

Lunch in hand, Gold pushed out the door and ran into someone.

"I'm so sorry," she apologized, clutching the person's arm.

Her reflection stared back at her in the mirrored sunglasses, but the mouth above the scarf curved upward.

"The fault is entirely mine." He bent to retrieve her bag and handed it to her. "I must say it's never a bad thing to run into a beautiful woman."

"Thanks," Gold murmured, suddenly wary. She wasn't sure why, but this man put her on the defensive. He was smiling, but it wasn't quite genuine.

"I hope I didn't damage your lunch."

"Not at all." She brushed aside the concern. When she sidestepped to go around the stranger, he moved with her.

Alarm bells rattled, and she slipped her free hand in her pocket, where she kept a can of pepper spray.

"You're Troy's lady, right?"

"Who's asking?" She tightened her fingers around the little canister and backed up a step. There was just enough room for her to dart back into the building and go out a different way if need be. Or kick him in the balls.

"Give him a message for me. Time is running out."

Before she could respond, a group of college students moved in, and the man was lost in the crowd. With her head on the swivel, she hurried back to her office. She closed and locked the door, then raced to her office.

There she dialed her father's number.

⌒

"What do you mean you don't know what he looks like?" her father demanded. "I trained you better than that!"

They now sat in the room Gold used for group therapy sessions. Now it was set up with three long tables in a u shape with chairs on the outside. Falls paced while Gold slumped in one of the chairs. Her lunch sat forgotten on the table at her elbow.

"Help me help you," her father pleaded.

Gold rubbed her temples. Her pulse still hadn't stopped racing and if she wasn't mistaken, the earlier adrenaline rush was wearing off and her mood was plummeting. It probably didn't help she still hadn't eaten her lunch. "Dad, he was wearing sunglasses, a hat, and leather gloves," she answered wearily. "He was light skinned, no facial hair. And he was nauseatingly polite."

"That's not enough information," he complained.

Again, she rubbed her temples. What else had she noticed about the man? Closing her eyes, she tugged on her memory. She wasn't paying much attention, thinking only about Troy. That brought a smile even as she worried her lower lip. Okay, cold air as she opened the door. Stepped outside and right into the man. Wait...

"He was waiting for me." A chill went through her. "He made sure I ran into him."

A clatter outside drew their attention to the door. A moment later, it opened and Troy wheeled in. His frantic gaze bounced around the room before settling on Gold. Relief washed over his features.

"You're okay."

Before he could cross the distance, Falls stalked to the man and jerked him up by his lapels.

"What the hell have you gotten my daughter involved in?" he demanded.

"Dad!" Gold exclaimed, jumping to her feet. "Stop!" She rushed to her father, trying in vain to pry his fingers from Troy's coat.

"I should run you in." Falls shook the younger man.

Troy grasped Falls's wrists as he gained his feet. There was no way in the world he was going to hit Gold's father, but the man was coming awfully close to getting popped in the jaw. Instead, Troy reversed the wrist lock, surprising Falls with the move. Troy stumbled back, lost his balance, and collapsed to the floor.

Gold knelt beside him. "Are you hurt?" She ran her hands over his body, anxiously checking for any bruises.

He chuckled. "It's been a while since an angry father caught me off guard."

Gold stood, bracing her feet as she helped Troy to stand. He wobbled. She moved to help him, but he waved her off. So, she grabbed his chair and brought it to him.

"I did some checking..." Falls began.

Gold whirled, hands on hips and fire in her eyes. "How dare you!" she sputtered. "I'm trying to figure out if the display you showed me was my dad or the cop."

Falls glared at his daughter. "Both." He shifted the steely gaze to Troy. "Mind telling me why some stranger is accosting my daughter on the streets?"

Troy locked gazes with Gold. "You didn't tell me you were threatened." He kept his voice low.

"He didn't threaten me. Well, not in words; it was his manner."

Troy wheeled closer, taking her hand in his. He didn't like how it trembled.

"If he didn't threaten you with words, what did he say?" Falls jumped in.

With her free hand, Gold rubbed her temple.

Troy glanced around the room and spied the brown paper bag on the table. "Is that your lunch?" He placed her hand on his shoulder as he moved toward the table.

"We don't have time for this."

"Then make time!" Troy snapped. Gentling his voice, he said, "Sit down, sweetheart."

Gold sank into the leather office chair as Troy opened the bag and removed the still warm pie. He unwrapped the foil and was met with fragrant steam. His own stomach rumbled.

"Smells delicious."

She shook her head. "I'm too upset to eat," she murmured.

He cocked his head, scooping up a spoonful of the crust and chicken. "Take a bite for me," he coaxed.

Falls observed the two. On one hand, he wanted to go pound the young man in the wheelchair who was bossing him around. Yet, as he watched, there was so much tenderness and care in the way he treated Gold. Falls knew Troy's background. The guy was clean, other than a few parking tickets, but who didn't have those? He was definitely in a way better position than the last man Gold dated, but Falls had been so afraid for his daughter. So a man comes up to her and scares her. No one was going to do that to his little girl.

"What exactly did he say?" Troy was asking. He held another spoonful of food to Gold.

Gold kept her gaze on Troy, even though she directed her answer to Falls. "He asked if I was Troy's lady." She chewed and swallowed. "At that point, I was pretty defensive and had my pepper spray ready. He said to give Troy a message."

"What was the message?" Falls demanded.

Troy flashed him a scathing look. Gold smiled. "It's okay. I'm calmer now." She dabbed her mouth with the napkin, surprised to see she'd eaten the entire pie.

"You just needed to eat," Troy assured her. He rested a hand on her thigh. "Keep talking."

"The man said time is running out."

Chapter Seven

Troy stared out the window at the unbroken site of the field adjacent to his backyard. Barren trees raised their naked limbs to the white and gray sky. A few days had passed since Gold's run-in with the man. Even with her father pulling surveillance tapes from the area, there was still no way to identify him. Yet somehow Troy thought this had to be related to what he'd done for his cousin. But all Troy had done was store something in his safe deposit box. It wasn't the first time he'd done so. So, whatever the man wanted, Troy no longer had, and there was no way he could get a message to his cousin.

He rubbed the bridge of his nose. What had he seen that day? Danta had removed a stick of chewing gum from the small envelope. Troy wasn't sure why his cousin had him store something so mundane. Could that be what the man was after?

Light footsteps creaked behind him. Troy turned to find Gold making her way to him. She was dressed in one of his tee shirts again. Her long curly hair was swept into a puff ball on the top of her hair, making her look more like a teen than a grown woman.

"I'm sorry about my dad." She settled in one corner of the couch, folding her legs beneath her.

Troy snagged a fuzzy blanket from an ottoman as he passed. He spread it over Gold. "Your dad loves you, and he's protective of you. Same as me."

Gold snuggled into the blanket. "I've never seen him like that before. Did he hurt you?"

Troy laughed. "It takes more than that to hurt me." He smiled. "Most people wouldn't have come after me like he did."

Gold managed a rueful smile. "He hangs around Father Time a lot. Dad doesn't distinguish between disabled and able-bodied people. He's an equal opportunity ass kicker." She rubbed her cheek on the blanket. "You did surprise him though."

Troy moved to sit next to her, placing an arm over her shoulders. "How so?"

"He's used to people being cowed by his badge. You did neither. In fact, you snapped at him."

"You were hurting right then, and he was only adding to it," he answered a bit defensively.

She laughed. "Don't ever apologize for caring for me. If you hadn't been there, I know I wouldn't have eaten, and the drop would've been a lot worse."

"You're feeling better now?"

Nodding, she shifted until she could rest her head on his shoulder. "Being close to you helps."

They fell silent, watching the world outside the window. The endless expanse of white was so pretty, even this late in the season.

"Valentine's Day is coming," Troy began. "Anything special you'd like to do?"

"You're asking me to be your Valentine?"

"You are the only woman I want as my Valentine."

Softly, she kissed him. "You make me feel like the most cherished person."

"You are."

She stroked his face. "There's something you're not telling me."

He stiffened.

She chuckled. "You've a protective streak a mile wide and I admire that, but when we were in my office that day, you had this look on your face. You looked," she paused as she searched for the word. "Guilty."

"Let me start by saying I don't know who the man was. If I did, I would tell you and your father."

"Okay."

"The only thing I can think of is it may have something to do with a family member who has passed away."

"I'm sorry." She covered his hand with hers.

He shook his head. "I stored some items for him before he passed away. A few weeks ago, I passed them to a friend of his." Troy sent up a prayer of forgiveness for twisting the truth. He couldn't totally betray his cousin, but he could give Gold a little of the truth while keeping her safe. "That's the only thing I can think of that maybe this guy wants."

Gold bit her bottom lip. "Could you get it back?"

"No."

"Do you know what it was?"

"My cousin handed me a sealed envelope. I never looked in it."

"Who was your cousin?"

"Sam Goodwin"

Gold sat up straight. "Sam? He was your cousin?" she demanded. "I knew him. He was a great therapist. As a matter of fact, I have a few of his patients." Tears welled in her eyes. "He was a very compassionate, caring man. And the way he died only made it worse."

Troy ducked his head. She'd known Sam, or Danta as he was known now. He had to keep his cousin's secret for all their sakes.

"We used to talk every day," he admitted. "And helped me get my mental straight when I had to rely more on being in a wheelchair. He kept reminding me life was not over, just different."

"Exactly. I tell myself the same thing when I feel down about not driving anymore." She squeezed his hand. "I know it's not the same."

"It's a loss of some of your independence," he surmised.

"Yes." Relief washed through her. He did understand.

"How do you deal with it, Gold? You have a lot more sight than many of your friends. How do you keep your optimism?"

She pondered this moment. "The hardest thing has been not driving. Being more intentional in my plans has been an adjustment since I'm not able to jump in the car and go whenever the whim strikes. On the flip side, I can get emails and documentation done while I'm riding. I couldn't do that before, well, at least not safely."

He chuckled.

"Then when I look at my friends Penelope and Geneva, who are thriving, why in the world should I feel like my life is over? Geneva was born without eyes, and Penelope and I have the same eye condition."

"Oh really?"

She nodded. "Just different aspects of it. I have a form of retinitis pigmentosa, called Nystagmus, which causes the eye to jump around. There are still days where I have to remind myself that not everyone sees like I do." She stared into the distance. "I wish I'd known Sam was your cousin sooner."

"You know now. That's what is important."

Troy sat on the workout bench, arms outstretched to the side as he lifted and lowered a pair of 25-lb. dumbbells. He'd been at his workout for the last forty-five minutes and was covered in sweat. The cotton shirt he wore was soaked through. With a grunt and a groan, he set the weights on the rubberized floor. He then picked up a thick elastic cord, kept his hands out in front of him, and pulsed the bands enough to keep them tight. He did several reps until his shoulders screamed and burned, then did another fifteen reps. Tossing the bands aside, he reached for a bottle of water and drank deeply.

A few other people were in the gym, but they were in their own worlds. A woman with a high ponytail, earbuds in, ran on a treadmill. Another patron utilized the rowing machine and the last pair, another trainer and an older man, were going through a set of ab exercises. Troy set down his water, picked up the weights, and then returned them to the stand.

A blast of cold air pushed the humid, sweatiness around, and Troy looked up to greet the newcomer.

A woman dressed in a long dark trench coat, shades, and a fur-trimmed cap strolled in on a pair of high-heeled boots. She paused long enough to survey the room before working her way toward him. He didn't see a duffle bag, or anything slung over her shoulder, so she couldn't be here for a workout. Then again, she could be here for a consultation. Yet as she approached, she didn't smile or remove her sunglasses. A whisper of unease drifted over him.

"You've done well for yourself," she greeted.

"Do I know you?" he queried, moving back slightly so he didn't have to crane his neck to maintain eye contact.

"No, but you took something not belonging to you." She shifted.

Troy caught a whiff of antiseptic, as if she'd been in the hospital or doctors' office. Maybe she was a little deranged? "Lady, you need to leave. I don't have time for your issues." He gestured toward the door.

Now she smiled, but it wasn't pleasant. "This is a really nice place you have here."

"I think you need to leave." He couldn't quite put his finger on it, but this woman was threatening him, and he didn't like it.

"I'm sorry. I thought we were having a pleasant conversation, Mr. Curtis."

"You see, I never told you my name and when someone smiles like you do, no good can come of it. You'll need to leave."

"You have something of mine," she said, as she paced his chair.

"I don't have anything of yours," he snapped.

She put a hand on his chair, halting his forward motion. "You see, I know where you got the money to start this gym and for your rehabilitation."

Troy carefully removed the woman's hand from his chair and wheeled out of her range. "You know nothing," he stated coldly. "Now leave before I call the cops and have you arrested for trespassing."

She nodded. "Fine. Then we'll do this the hard way. Remember you were warned." She turned on a heel and strolled out.

Troy gripped the chair arms as he stared after her. She knew his name and where he worked. Coupled with the few threatening phone calls and the intimidation of Gold, he had no doubt this had something to do with what his cousin had given him to store in his safety deposit box.

Troy frowned. He no longer had anything from his cousin. If anything, why now? Why were these people coming after him now? What changed? He wheeled to the waist-high check-in counter. Once behind the furniture, he searched the shelves for a small phonebook. In the digital age when everyone Googled people, places, and things, he still liked to let his fingers do the walking. He found the number and placed a call to a detective agency. As he listened to the ringing on the other end, he wondered if he should give Gold's father a call too. Maybe if he explained the situation, the officer might have some insight.

If what he had to say got him arrested, then so be it. He would not put Gold in danger and not know why. He hung up the phone, then dialed Sgt. Falls.

⌒

Twenty minutes later, the two men sat at a table. Menus sat untouched on the wooden surface while glasses of ice water waited on coasters.

"I asked you here because I got a visit from a woman threatening me." Troy sipped the water. "I've also been getting phone calls telling me I'm running out of time."

Falls sat studying Troy with an unreadable expression. "Do you know who these people are?"

Troy shook his head. "I think it has something to do with my cousin."

"Was your cousin some sort of thug?" There was a slight bite to the question.

"No, he was murdered in a botched bank robbery."

The older man's face softened. "I'm sorry to hear that. When?"

"Earlier this year. It happened at downtown Flint."

Falls held up a hand. "I remember something about that. A couple of people died during that robbery." Falls pulled out his phone, typed a moment, then looked up. "Your cousin was the shrink."

"Yes."

"Interesting he happened to be in Flint when we have a perfectly good branch of the same bank right here in Ann Arbor."

"My cousin volunteered somewhere there in the city. If he had banking to do, it makes sense."

"All right." He paused as the waiter approach. They ordered. Once the server left, Falls resumed. "So, what makes you think this has something to do with your cousin?"

This was the tricky part. He had to make it seem like he'd given the envelope to someone other than his cousin. "These people think I have something of theirs."

"Do you?"

Troy shook his head. "No."

"If you don't have it, why do they think you do?"

He shrugged. "I don't know what this is about. My main concern is for Gold. I don't want her to get hurt because of some perceived item I don't have."

"Did you ever have it?"

Startled, Troy didn't answer.

Falls nodded wisely. "I see." He sipped his own water. "What did you do with the item?"

"Turned it over to his estate."

Falls raised a brow. "Somehow I don't believe you."

He shrugged. "The fact is I no longer have the item. I never knew what it was."

"Now that I do believe."

"Look Sarge, I love your daughter and will do anything to protect her. I'm bringing this to you because she is vulnerable, and I don't want anything to happen to her."

Falls studied the man before him for a long moment. "Does Gold know how you feel about her?"

"I haven't told her in those exact words," he admitted bashfully.

"When my daughter told me she was dating you, I looked into your background."

"As expected." The invasion of his privacy, though expected, still chafed.

"You got a bum deal." Falls nodded to indicate the wheelchair Troy sat in. "The way the company and the CEO wiggled out of the lawsuits associated with the accident, which help put you in that chair. How many people died in the accident?"

"Too many," Troy answered stiffly. While he'd told Gold his necessity for a wheelchair was due to lupus, yes, in part it was true, the main reason he was dependent on this chair was due to a partial building collapse aggravated by a car accident.

The building would've eventually failed, due to poor workmanship the architect and builder were fully aware of, but also the car in question, which had plowed into the building, had substantial recalls on the steering and brake systems. All of those culminated into the perfect storm. While he was confined to a wheelchair, many more had lost their lives, including the woman and daughter in the vehicle.

"You did receive a settlement of sorts shortly after the trial," Falls continued.

"Which will never be enough to compensate for the perpetual pain I suffer every day," he cut in. "I'm asking for your help in keeping Gold safe."

"She would be safe had you not entered her life."

Troy opened his mouth to protest, then stopped. Falls had a point. "Neither of us can unring that bell. Now do I have your help or not?"

⌐

"Oh, my goodness! Geneva is going to love this!" Gold exclaimed, running her fingers along the sequined tablecloth. Another held raised rosettes. A rainbow of pastel bows adorned the chair covers. Each of the centerpieces was an arrangement of items new parents would need for their baby. Everything from diapers and bottles to little onesies and socks. Gold stepped closer to one table to examine the trio of bathing supplies—baby shampoo, wash, and lotion were arranged in a small basket, along with washcloths and several hooded bath towels. She fingered one, yearning stretched through her. What would it be like if she had a little one of her own? Would Troy even want children?

Truthfully that was something they hadn't discussed. If anything, they hadn't gotten beyond exchanging keys to each other's homes. Gold spent more time at Troy's home, as it provided more privacy than her condo near the mall. Not that the walls were thin at her place, but there was something liberating about being in a freestanding dwelling getting her ass spanked than in her apartment. Someone could get the wrong idea at the noises on the other side of the door.

A slow smile creased her lips at the thought of a neighbor interrupting their play time.

"Do you really think she'll be surprised?" Jethro asked anxiously. He straightened one of the pink bows on the back of a satin clad chair.

"She's going to love this," Gold assured him. "She's due in a couple of weeks, right?"

Jethro nodded. "Yes. Our parents are on standby. My dad helped assemble the crib last week." He moved forward, clicking his tongue as he went.

Gold smiled. She always admired Jethro for his ability to use echolocation, which was using sounds to determine where obstacles were located. He seldom used a white cane— the mobility device that most blind or visually impaired individuals used to navigate their environment. Her vision hadn't deteriorated to the point of utilizing a white cane, but soon she would need one. Truth be told, she could use one now, but pride and stubbornness kept her from using it.

"So tomorrow afternoon, we'll get her out of the house and finish up any decorations before we bring her here."

"That's the plan."

"Thank you for helping me pull this off," Jethro said. "We've wanted a baby for so long and now we're having one, it seems so surreal."

"Well, you have a lot of friends and family to help."

"I know. I just don't think I'm ready to be a father," he responded ruefully.

Gold bit back a laugh. "Well, ready or not, your little bundle of joy will be here soon. Good thing is you and Geneva have lots of love to give and that's what babies need."

In a rare display of emotion, Jethro hugged Gold. "Thanks. You've been a really good friend through all of this."

She patted his back. "You're welcome." She pushed the button on her watch to announce the time. "I've gotta run. I've got a session in about twenty minutes."

Bundled against the cold, Gold hurried up the salt-encrusted walk the four blocks or so to her office. Valentine's Day was just around the corner, and Troy had something planned. She paused for the crosswalk, moving until her shoes met the bump dots, signaling the start of the curb. Once the red hand flashed to a white light, Gold continued across the red bricks to the other side.

Frankly, she thought he was taking her to a spanking party for the weekend. She'd never been to one and thought it would be great fun. And it would be the perfect outing to celebrate their decision to be an exclusive couple. Crossing the final street to her block, Gold hurried into the warmth with a grateful sigh. She paused as her glasses fogged up.

"Two of the group are already here," Stacy, the receptionist, announced. "You still have about ten minutes before you need to start."

Gold nodded. "Good. Gives me time to catch my breath."

"Your father is waiting in your office for you."

Frowning, Gold moved toward her office. Her father sat on the sofa she kept for clients. There was also an armchair and a side table with a box of tissues. Gold took her time hanging up her outer wear. She closed the door. "Is everything all right?"

"I wanted to check on you." He stood, crossed the room, and kissed her cheek.

"I was at Abigail's Place with Jethro. We were going over last-minute things for Geneva's baby shower."

"Did Troy ever tell you how he came to be in a wheelchair?"

"Yes. What's your reason for asking?"

"Was wondering how honest he's been with you."

Gold barely refrained from rolling her eyes. "Dad, if anything, you've taught me to ask the questions I want answers to."

"He knows why someone tried scaring you when you were at lunch."

"Yes. He told me some people think he has something he no longer has."

Falls gasped.

She smiled. "You thought he was keeping me in the dark?" She shook her head. "He worries about me, Dad. Troy makes sure I'm safe, healthy, happy, and cherished. Having a man I love do those things without asking has been a dream of mind. I know he doesn't tell me everything, nor do I want him to tell me everything."

"You're in love with him."

She offered a little laugh. "I guess I am."

Falls sat in the chair closest to the desk. "Are you sure about him, sweetheart? He's in a wheelchair, and you're losing your sight. Neither one of you has what could be a normal life. Are you ready for the challenges that come with your respective conditions?" he asked gently.

"You didn't seem to have a problem snatching him out of his chair."

Falls winced. "Not my finest moment, but I'd do it again."

She gave him a quick hug. "I love you, Dad. Troy is a lot like you; you both will do anything to protect me."

He smiled before his expression turned serious. "He asked me to help keep an eye on you."

Gold sat back. "The man who threatened me wasn't an isolated incident."

"Correct. Troy was threatened again today."

Gold gasped, clamping a hand over her mouth, as if to push the exclamation back. She rushed to her coat, fumbling in the pocket to retrieve her phone. Behind her, clothing rustled. Strong hands rested on her shoulders.

"He's okay."

Gold blinked rapidly to contain the burn of tears. Still, her hands shook as she looked at the screen on her phone. There were a couple of text messages waiting. She tapped them. Both were from Troy. The first said, "I'm fine," and the second read, "Call me when you get this."

She closed her eyes and breathed.

"Gold?" her father queried.

She bobbed her head. "I'm okay. Just give me a moment." She pulled off her glasses to wipe her damp eyes. "You said he called you? So, you saw him today?"

"Right before I came to see you," he promised. "He was absolutely fine. Well, very concerned for you."

"I need to talk to him."

Falls nodded. "Call me when you're done for the day. I'll swing by and take you home."

She glanced at the clock. "I should be done by four."

"I'll see you at fifteen after then." He kissed her cheek. "Now don't be late for your next appointment."

Absently, Gold waved as she dialed Troy's number. "Are you okay?" she demanded as soon as he answered.

"Yes," he replied, a bit breathless.

She dabbed at the tears rolling down her cheeks. "My dad said someone threatened you."

"Yes. I called your father because I don't want anything to happen to you. Just a moment." Clothing rustled and his voice muffled. "Did two miles on the treadmill."

Gold flicked a glance at the clock. She was already five minutes late.

"Sorry about that. I'm with a client, but I wanted to make sure you knew I was okay."

Relief flooded her, making her knees weak. "I'm glad you did. I'm late for my next session. Can we talk over dinner? My dad will bring me home."

"I promise to explain as much as I can. I need you to understand why all of this is happening."

"I love you, Troy."

His smile crackled in her ear. "I love you too, Gold."

She leaned her head against her closed door and breathed. Once she found her calm, she slipped her phone in her pocket, picked up a pen and notepad, and went to the conference room.

Before she turned the corner, happy laughter floated through the open door. A smile teased her lips. The group sounded upbeat. The metallic jingle of dog tags interspersed with the muted voices and occasional giggles. She stepped inside and closed the door.

"Sorry I'm late," she began. "Had to advert a mini crisis."

"You're human, ya know," Penelope teased.

"GG was just telling us about the time the health inspector visited Jason," August supplied.

"Oh?" Gold prompted, settling into her chair.

As before, GG, August, Penelope, Abigail, Amelia, and Geneva sat in a semi-circle. All the women were smiles today, whether from the anecdote from GG or whether life was dishing out the best chocolates, the women before her were relaxed and smiling.

"Yes. When the truck was being sabotaged, the health inspector came to check us out. He asked Jason how he knew what the temps were, since he couldn't read the numbers. When Jason showed him, the man nodded. Jason called him in on it and the look on the guy's face was priceless. A combination of 'Oh shit, I'm a moron' and 'Oh shit, this guy can't see me' nod."

A hearty chuckle went through the room.

"I love when that happens," Abigail remarked.

"My favorite is when the children educate the parents on how to act," Geneva said. "When we did White Cane Awareness, I had a fan ask for my autograph. Her mother asked how could I sign when I can't see. Or children tell their parents not to pet the dog because she's working," Amelia added.

"We can do everything but drive."

"Samson disabled a bomb," August stated with nonchalance. "Not an experience I'd like to repeat."

"The last thing we are is helpless," Penelope declared.

Gold grinned. She loved this group. They were more than just her patients; they were her friends. And again, she was reminded in spite of the challenges these women faced, they were happy.

"So, does anyone have anything new to share? Any gripes from the past week? Or comments?"

"I'm giving serious consideration to asking Samson to marry me," August admitted.

A murmur of approval rolled through the women. GG reached over and touched August's hand.

"Really?" GG squealed. "Stx is so into you, and he'll have you no matter what, but I know he really wants to show you how committed he is by having you as his wife."

"Can you tell me your thought process behind this decision, August?" Gold queried. "You've made it known several times you weren't interested in a traditional relationship per se."

Indeed, August wasn't. She practiced polyamory—maintaining multiple ethical relationships with more than two persons. After her divorce several years ago, she vowed not to give any one man that type of power over her again, instead choosing to love multiple men and enjoying her choice.

"Nearly dying," August confessed. "Samson deserves to have all of his heart's desires just as I do. The one thing he desires is to be my husband."

"Do you think marrying him will change your love style?" Gold probed.

August tilted her head, considering. "No, but I am concerned it may change our dynamic."

"How so? Samson has been very open to your love style this long. How do you think it would change?"

Shouting filtered through the closed door.

"What's going on?" Penelope asked.

"Sit tight a moment." Gold set her pad and pen on her empty chair, then crossed the room.

A thud vibrated the walls. Before she could touch the doorknob, the wood was flung open. The edge of the door caught her on the side of the head, and she tumbled backward. Pain slashed through her head, and she cried out.

"Nobody move." The male voice ordered low and menacing.

Cries and sobs of distress whimpered through the room.

Gold slowly sat up, touching the knot on her head. Her fingertips came away wet, and her glasses were askew.

"Whatever you need, let me help," Gold said in a calm, soothing voice. Inside, she was shaking. How dare this man come into her office, frighten her friends, and lord knows what else.

"Do exactly what I say, and no one gets hurt." He reached down and yanked Gold unceremoniously to her feet. She dug in her heels. Yes, he was bigger and stronger than she was, but could she disarm him without getting anyone else hurt in the process? Inhaling a breath, she jabbed an elbow in his gut. Air left his lungs with a whoosh! For added measure she stomped his instep with her heel as hard as she could. He grunted but it barely loosened his hold. Balling her fist, she brought it down and into his crotch. Now he howled, releasing her. She scurried forward aiming for her office and her cell phone.

The victory was short lived when a heavy body slammed her into the wall. For a brief moment she saw stars as she gasped for breath. Cruel fingers bit into her hair as hot, fetid breath blew in her face. "Do that again and I promise

I'll go back in there and shoot every pregnant woman in the stomach."

Cold anger tightened her gut. "You're despicable."

"Do I have your cooperation or do I go back and start shooting?"

What could she do? Even if the threat was only there to garner her cooperation, she couldn't risk any of the others being hurt. Bitter tears burned her eyes and she angrily blinked them back. "Fine," she said through gritted teeth.

He transferred his hold to her arm. "Now let's go!"

Gold winced as his iron grip bit the circulation off in her arm. She stumbled as he propelled her forward. There had to be something she could do. Each time she hesitated, he jerked her forward. Maybe she could start a rapport? "What's your name?" she asked. The least she could do was try to humanize them both, establish a rapport so he would find it harder to hurt her later.

"You don't need to know, Doc." He jabbed his weapon into her ribs.

"Ow!"

He pushed her down the hall and into the reception area. Stacy laid crumpled on the floor, halfway behind the desk. Gold made a move toward her and was yanked back.

"But she's hurt," Gold snapped.

"Not as hurt as she could be if you help her," the man threatened.

He shoved her out the door. The cold barely registered as he shoved her toward a waiting sedan. Gold slipped in an icy patch but was held upright by the savage grip on her arm. She cast up and down the street for any help. For once, the way was quiet. No cars, no pedestrians, not even a newspaper tumbleweed.

With his other hand, he opened the door. "Get in."

Gold hesitated. If she got in the car, would she have enough time to dive out while he made his way around the driver's side?

As if sensing her thoughts, he poked her with the gun. "Climb over the console. You're driving."

"But I...."

"Get the fuck in the car!"

Without another word, Gold climbed in, navigated the center console, and then settled in the driver's seat. By now, her teeth were chattering. She glanced over the steering wheel. This was a newer sedan with the push button ignition and a knob to place the car in gear.

Presuming he had the key fob, she mashed the brake pedal and pushed the start button. The car whispered to life. Gold hadn't driven in the last six months. She lamented her failing eyesight and the loss of driving independence. Now she was being forced to drive at gunpoint.

With some trepidation, she eased the car onto the vacant road. Tension stretched and strained through every nerve ending. She constantly checked the road, side mirrors, and speedometer. There weren't even cops patrolling the area. She stifled a hysterical giggle. Gold had to rein it in or would lose it before they even got to where they were going. How is it no one was out on the day she needed to signal for help?

"I really shouldn't be driving," she began conversationally. "I'm actually legally blind, and it really isn't safe for me to drive."

"You're doing just fine," the man grunted.

"What should I call you? Mr. Thug?"

"Listen, Doc, call me whatever you like. I've done this a time or two, and I have no qualms about killing you," he explained. "So do your little psycho-babble therapist bull-shit all you want. I get paid whether you're dead or alive."

Gold swallowed hard. This man was motivated by money, so if words wouldn't sway him, maybe she could make him a better offer. "How much are you getting paid?" She braked for a yellow light.

The man flashed a feral, white smile. "I've already checked your net worth, Doc. You ain't got the capital."

The light turned green, and she stepped on the gas. Could she crash the car? "Is there a particular destination you have in mind, or do I need to keep driving aimlessly through the streets of Ann Arbor?"

"You drive until I tell you to stop."

Chapter Eight

"What do you mean she's gone?" Troy demanded. He swung his gaze from Sgt. Falls to Det. Potter.

"I need you to remain calm right now," Falls told him.

Troy scanned the room. They were in the corridor outside Gold's office. Magazines and papers were scattered on the floor. A few of the pictures lining the wall were knocked askew, while a few drops of a reddish-brown substance, which he suspected may be blood dotted the floor. Not enough to indicate someone was dying, but enough to know a struggle had ensued. A wisp of pride filled him. His Gold had fought back. Then his gaze landed on her coat and bag. They were still in the room. Someone had taken her outside without a coat; she would be freezing. Anguish squeezed his heart. This was his fault. He had no idea where Gold could be, but he knew beyond a doubt this was his fault.

A paramedic knelt on the floor next to Stacy. He squeezed the bulb on a blood pressure cuff while he listened to the pulses with the stethoscope. With the task completed, he took her pulse. He glanced at the cops. "We'll take her in for observation but go ahead and ask her your questions."

Falls read the name tag. "Jeffries. Thanks. Give us a moment."

Stacy lifted tear-filled eyes to him. "He came in like he was a new patient," Stacy explained. "When I told him Dr. Falls was in session, he got belligerent. I think I yelled at him when he started to go back. When I tried to stop him, he hit me."

"You have surveillance, right?" Potter demanded.

Stacy pointed to a monitor near her desk. "It backs up to the cloud. There's no need for tapes or whatnot."

A bell tinkled, and several pairs of heavy feet pounded down the hall. Five men pushed their way into the corridor. Their concerned voices echoed and bounced off the walls and ceiling. A nearby door opened.

"We're fine," GG sang out. "Just a little shaken."

The newcomers flowed around Troy, Falls, and Potter to the conference room. Each going to their respective woman. Jethro wrapped his arms around Geneva, holding her trembling body close to his as she sobbed into his chest. He murmured soothing words in her ear as he stroked her back.

"Amelia," Joshua Hastings caressed a faint scar near Amelia's hairline before he skimmed her lips with a kiss.

She clung to him. "I'm okay. Still trying to process what happened."

"P." Avery gathered Penelope close, his hand resting on her swollen belly.

"We're fine," she said wearily. "The man didn't even come in the room."

GG hurried to where Jason stood, wrapped her arms around his waist. "I'm not hurt," she assured him.

Swift Time strolled toward Abigail. "Hey there, lover."

Abigail ringed her arms around Time's neck. "I'm so glad you're here. I don't understand why things like this keep happening to us."

"You're safe," he soothed.

"Sol?" Samson called out. "Where's Sol?"

August touched his hand; that was enough for him to draw her close and kiss her soundly.

"I'm fine."

"Well, I'm not," he replied.

She disentangled from his arms and went to one knee.

"What are you doing?" he demanded.

"I'm down on one knee, asking you to marry me," she said.

"Now?" he asked incredulously. "You pick now to ask me."

"Now is as good a time as any. If we wait, neither one of us will be alive to get married."

He drew her to her feet. "Of course I'll marry you."

They kissed to a smattering of applause.

"Now that we've got the romantic stuff out the way, could we get back to the problem at hand?" Potter demanded.

"Young man, why are you always so surly?" Time wanted to know. "Dr. Falls is just fine."

"How do you know this?"

"If Time says Gold is fine, then she is," Falls stated. He sank into a nearby chair.

GG stepped over to the men. She held Jason's hand.

"Sgt. Falls. Troy," she began. "Everything happened really fast. We heard shouting, a thud. Gold went to the door to make sure everything was all right. The man came in. He hit her with the door. I saw her fall, and the next thing I know he's dragging her out of here at gunpoint."

"Are you sure?" Falls said.

She nodded. "He forced her to drive."

"What kind of car was it?"

She smiled. "I can do one better." She fished a slip of paper from her pocket and handed it to him. "I got the license plate number."

Gold squinted in the waning light. The gray light of dusk always messed with her vision There was neither enough light to see or too much light to make out objects. There had to be a way she could use this to her advantage. A quick glance to her right confirmed the man still did not wear a seatbelt. He'd also lowered the gun to a non-lethal level and hadn't given her any directions to a specific place.

She made a left turn on Zeeb Rd where it crossed Jackson. Meijer grocery store was on her right and a Burger King on her left. She stayed in the far left-hand lane, knowing the right would eventually end. There were a number of two-lane roads where her plan could work. As a matter of fact, she could swing by the Pittsfield Library. There were open fields and a concrete barrier she could use. She made another right and paused at the light.

Glancing to her left, she made sure there were no lights headed her way. She peeled her fingers from the steering wheel long enough to wipe her sweaty hands on her jeans. She gunned the engine as she keeled the wheel hard right.

"Stop it."

"I intend to." She aimed the sedan toward the barrier for the guardrails. At the last minute, she swerved enough to the right for the right side of the vehicle to collide with the barrier. Metal crunched and squealed as it twisted along the guardrail.

A bright flash of light blinded Gold as shrieks and breaking glass filled the interior. Pain bloomed along her thigh, and she cried out as her leg spasmed in response.

Pale smoke exploded as the airbags deployed. The car slid, caught something on the front end, and then careened on its side. She smacked her head on the glass. Blackness encroached on her vision as the world went weightless.

Tires squealed. A horn blared, while voices shouted back and forth. She thought she heard a siren wail before she let unconsciousness embrace her.

Epilogue

"Surprise!" Several jubilant voices shouted.

"Definitely a surprise," Geneva remarked. She pressed her hands to her damp cheeks, wiping tears away. "I can't believe you guys did all this."

Jethro led her around the room. She oohed and ahhed over the textures of the tablecloths, chair covers, and sashes. She fingered one of the intricately tied bows.

"How did you do all this?"

"I had a lot of help," Jethro confessed.

From one corner of the room, Gold observed the happy parents-to-be. She touched the small bandage on her forehead and winced. The skin felt way too tight in that area, but a knot and a couple of stitches would do that. However, it definitely didn't drown out the constant pulse and burn of her leg. During the crash, a bullet grazed her leg, leaving a three-inch furrow on her outer thigh. There would be no squats until she had the stitches removed.

"Are you okay?" Troy whispered in her ear.

She leaned against him, elation rolling through her. She snuggled close, placing his arm around her shoulders. She then rested herself against his chest, lulled by the steady thu-thunk of his heart. Inhaling deeply, she took his scent of pine and man into her lungs. He'd been the first face she'd seen in the hospital emergency room that fateful day.

"I'm okay," she confirmed.

"You really need to be in bed," he admonished.

She kissed the underside of his jaw. "In a bit, I really wanted to be here for Geneva."

"Your friends are amazing," he told her. "When I got to your office yesterday," he paused to clear the emotion from his throat and didn't quite get it all, "I wanted to keep you safe." He cinched her tighter. "Your friends said you tried to protect them and were abducted instead."

She shook her head. "The guy was going to kill me no matter what," she confessed. "No matter what tactic I tried, he was only interested in achieving his goal so he could get paid."

Troy flinched. "I'm sorry, Gold."

She smiled up at him. "My abduction wasn't your fault. If anything, you gave my dad the information he needed to help find me."

He shook his head. "That was all GG. She ran out in enough time to get the license plate number."

Laughter split the room. Gold looked in the direction of her friends celebrating a new life. There they all were with their husbands and significant others. August was sandwiched between Samson and Jason, with GG on the right side of Jason. Penelope leaned against her husband Avery, while Amelia sat in Joshua's lap. Abigail and Time held hands while Jethro fed Geneva a cube of cheese. There would be some residual angst from yesterday's trauma, but for today they were celebrating life.

"You want what they have," Troy observed.

She jerked her gaze to his. "What makes you say that?"

"I've gotten to know you pretty well over these last few weeks, Gold. You have a need to belong and be cherished. No matter how hard I tried to deny what we have, you are the only woman I want in my life, my bed, and my dungeon." He fumbled in his pocket, held a diamond solitaire between his thumb and forefinger. "Marry me?"

Only then did she realize the room was completely silent. All the attention was focused on them. She studied him.

"What do you say about being my Valentine for the rest of our lives?"

"Yes!"

He slid the ring on the third finger of her left hand. She leaned forward and kissed him to uproarious applause.

Book Club Questions

1. One of the comments often made to the blind or visually impaired is "Well, you don't look blind." What characteristics do you associate with the blind or visually impaired?

2. What stereotypes about blindness did you have before reading this series, and how has reading this series broken these preconceived notions?

3. In this book, both Gold and Troy face challenges: Troy physical challenges due to a car accident and lupus; Gold visual challenges. Would you pursue a relationship with someone with challenges? Why or why not?

4. BDSM or some form of kink has been in a few of the books. How well do you think it added to the characters' POV? Do you think BDSM would be something you would try? Why or why not?

Author Bio

Lynn Chantale, a romance novelist, short story writer, and part-time background singer, has published many stories across several genres. Her works *include Sex, Lies, and Joysticks*, *True Detective Series*, and *Broken Lens,* to name a few.

When she's not actively planning world domination, she's dominating her household, family, and her cat, Shakespeare. You can visit her at any of her cyber haunts:

Website: https://www.thehouseoflynn.com
Twitter: https://twitter.com/lynnchantale
Amazon Author: https://www.amazon.com/author/lynnchantale
Facebook: https://www.facebook.com/LynnChantaleAuthor
Facebook Group Tale's Tells: https://www.facebook.com/groups/talestells
Instagram: https://www.instagram.com/lynn_chantale/
Youtube: https://www.youtube.com/channel/UCHbAParOHDB7cwfSwUtU3cA

More books from
4 Horsemen Publications

Romance

Ann Shepphird
The War Council

Emily Bunney
All or Nothing
All the Way
All Night Long: Novella
All She Needs
Having it All
All at Once
All Together
All for Her

KT Bond
Back to Life
Back to Love
Back at Last

Lynn Chantale
The Baker's Touch
Blind Secrets
Broken Lens
Blind Fury
Time Bomb

VIP's Revenge
Chef's Taste

Mandy Fate
Love Me, Goaltender
Captain of My Heart

Mimi Francis
Private Lives
Private Protection
Private Party
Run Away Home
The Professor
Our Two-Week, One-
Night Stand

Shae Coon
Bound in Love
Controlling Assets
For His Own Protection
Her Broken Pieces
The Roma's Claim
The Roma's Promise

LGBT Romance

Eskay Kabba
Hidden Love
Not So Hidden
Signs of Affection

Lucas LaMont
Roman's Reckoning: Type 6
Mikaél's Moment: Type 6
Stephan's Resurgence: Type 5
Anastasia's Arrival: Type 6

Stormie Skyes
Check Yes, No, or Maybe

Discover more at
4HorsemenPublications.com